Sonny stared at her for a moment before leading her back to the stairs to his apartment.

He opened the door and let her in. "You can take the bed—"

"I'll be fine on the sofa, thank you."

"Don't be ridiculous." He nearly scoffed.

"I'm not. You and I allowed ourselves to be baited into me staying here. This ridiculous situation is something I did to myself. You're...stuck in the middle. I'm not kicking you out of your bed. I'll sleep on the sofa and I'll be out of your life in the morning. My foot feels better—"

"Let's change that dressing." He motioned to the sofa. "Then I'll get you some sheets and a pillow."

"Okay." She considered it a win for her since her dressing needed to be changed by him regardless of where she slept. She sat on the sofa while Sonny knelt and changed the dressing, adding more haldi paste. He had a pleasant amount of scruff on his chin and thick hair that was tousled from the day. He smelled of spices. She inhaled deeply.

"This is healing nicely," he said.

She sat up straight, as if she had been caught doing something wrong. What was the matter with her? Or maybe the bigger question was, Why did he smell so good?

Dear Reader,

I am so thrilled that you've chosen *No Rings Attached*! This is the third book in my Once Upon a Wedding series. This one features a runaway bride! The idea came to me as I considered, What would happen if a bride ran from the mandap?

Sangeeta is extremely organized—she has a plan for everything! Her attention to detail and her natural tendency to think ahead mean she's a fabulous wedding planner, but when she runs from her wedding, no one really wants the Runaway Bride to plan *their* wedding.

As the oldest child, Sonny Pandya has been fixing his family's problems for as long as he can remember. He adores his younger siblings, Reena and Jai, and would do anything for them.

When Sangeeta turns up at his back door injured and in her wedding attire, he's flooded with a rush of memories from a year ago when they had spent a few fabulous days together. Against his better judgment, he helps her and then finds himself in a fake relationship with her to save his family's hotel, as well as Sangeeta's job.

If you've read the other books in this series, then you'll see some old friends! If not, go check them out after you've experienced Sonny and Sangeeta's journey. Each book stands alone, so no worries.

Please feel free to connect with me on Facebook at Facebook.com/monashroffauthor and Instagram @monashroffauthor, Twitter @monashroffwrite and TikTok @monaseesandwrites.

Best,

Mona Shroff

No Rings Attached

MONA SHROFF

HARLEQUIN
SPECIAL
EDITION

Recycling programs for this product may not exist in your area.

ISBN-13: 978-1-335-72460-1

No Rings Attached

Copyright © 2023 by Mona Shroff

For questions and comments about the quality of this book, please contact us at CustomerService@Harlequin.com.

Harlequin Enterprises ULC
22 Adelaide St. West, 41st Floor
Toronto, Ontario M5H 4E3, Canada
www.Harlequin.com

Printed in U.S.A.

Mona Shroff has always been obsessed with everything romantic, so it's fitting that she writes romantic stories by night, even though she's an optometrist by day. If she's not writing, she's likely to be making melt-in-your-mouth chocolate truffles, reading, or raising a glass of her favorite gin and tonic with friends and family. She's blessed with an amazing daughter and a loving son, who have both left the nest! Mona lives in Maryland with her romance-loving husband and their rescue dog, Nala.

Books by Mona Shroff

Harlequin Special Edition

Once Upon a Wedding

The Five-Day Reunion
Matched by Masala
No Rings Attached

Visit the Author Profile page
at Harlequin.com for more titles.

To my brother, Satyan Sharma.
I prayed for a little brother and my prayers were answered. To his wife, my sis-in-law, Monica Sharma. Be careful what you pray for. ;)

Acknowledgments

Every time I finish a book, I'm thoroughly amazed that I did it, but I never do it alone. Critique partner, brain stormer, author and friend extraordinaire Shaila Patel answers my texts and takes my calls when she should be working and all around helps me figure out what my characters are doing. Love you!

My editor, Susan Litman, guides me through the murky manuscript until it becomes a fabulous book. My agent, Rachel Brooks, cheers me on and supports me, with all my *still newbie* questions! I am always so grateful for you both.

A special thanks to the newest member of our family, Cole, for helping come up with the name of Sonny's restaurant, The Masala Hut, and for reading every book I write (some even twice!).

My friends and family, who have heard "But I'm on deadline" way too many times but still wait patiently while I do my thing, are precious to me in every way.

And of course, my partner in crime, Deven. It's been a fun ride so far. Let's see what happens next!

Chapter One

Sangeeta Parikh chuckled as her cousins Tina and Anita insisted on making infinitesimal adjustments to her panetar choli. A tiny pull here, a tuck there, yet another safety pin fastened. It wasn't even the full bridal sari—nobody wore that anymore—so there was really very little fussing that had to happen. Then they attacked her hair with more bobby pins, more powder, another coat of lip gloss, re-centering the chandlo, yet again. Sangeeta smiled to herself. This was how her cousins showed their love. They wanted her outfit, hair and makeup to be perfect. It was, after all, her wedding day.

She had planned it herself, but had asked her assistant, Toral, to work the events. Sangeeta closed her eyes and inhaled deeply, the light scent of jasmine from the flowers in her hair calming her.

Much to her mother's disappointment, Sangeeta had passed on the mehndi party as well as the garba. This was her wedding; she should be able to do what she wanted. And what Sangeeta wanted was a simple wedding, minimal fuss. She did not like being the center of attention, plain and simple. Her family had thought this was odd, and not just because she was a wedding planner. Any reason to party as far as they were concerned. But Sangeeta had insisted. The Ganesha puja had been at the crack of dawn this morning, so this was really the only major event—the wedding itself.

It occurred to her now that maybe she should have had Toral practice on a smaller event, just to be sure she knew the ropes and could handle the many little snafus that would always occur. People were unpredictable, and therefore, they were the actual wild card in any event, no matter how precisely planned.

She glanced at Toral. The woman, only a few years younger than Sangeeta, stood cool as a cucumber, dressed in a simple black blazer and a crisp white collared shirt tucked into black pants. Sangeeta had requested that Toral wear ballet flats as opposed to heels. They could not afford for anyone to be out because their feet hurt. Toral adjusted her headset as she tapped the iPad in front of her. Sangeeta saw Toral's lips move as she coordinated with the person they had inside the wedding hall.

Good. Toral had it under control. *Just like Sangeeta knew she would.*

Tina and Anita, her cousin and cousin-in-law, continued their air-primping, eyeing Sangeeta in the mirror.

"Toral will be fine handling things. She will not be

checking in with you. You need to focus on having fun, this is your *wedding*." Tina fixed her firm gaze on Sangeeta in the mirror. "How many do you plan on having?"

"Lip gloss," Anita commanded as she rummaged through the makeup bag.

"Her lip gloss is fine." Tina rolled her eyes. "Everything is fine. Sangeeta planned all of this—so it will be perfect."

Anita looked at Sangeeta in the mirror and smiled, Tina pulled a face, making Sangeeta laugh. These women anchored her, they were her family and she would be lost without them.

"Param is a lucky guy." Anita squeezed her arm.

"Damn straight he is." Tina kissed her cheek, leaving a light lipstick mark.

Sangeeta's stomach sank a bit, and her heart did a small tug at the thought of her husband-to-be, Param. The groom. Who was waiting for her in the mandap. Right now.

The man she would be spending the rest of her life with.

Nerves. It was nerves. Happened to every bride. At least that's how it seemed from the weddings she had planned. More than one bride had had serious nerves prior to walking down the aisle. And she'd talked them down from the ledge, every time.

So why did this feel so…different?

"My stomach is—"

"Doing flips?" laughed Tina.

"Filled with butterflies?" Anita said with a smirk.

Sangeeta furrowed her brow. "Well—" *Filled with dread.*

"It's all normal." Anita hugged her, looking at their reflection in the mirror. "Once you get down there, and see him, you'll see that you're both in this thing together. You're not alone."

Tina nodded agreement on her other side. "Look at how cute we are. We need a selfie." She grabbed her phone and they all turned toward the phone and took the selfie. Sangeeta forced a smile. She looked ill in the picture. Which made her panic more. Did brides have to force themselves to smile? Shouldn't it come naturally? Genuine smiles, from love?

"You got lipstick on her," Anita chided as she wiped at Sangeeta's cheek.

"She's fine." Tina shook her head at Anita.

A knock on the door had all three women turning to it. Toral calmly walked over and opened it, revealing one of Param's cousins. He was dressed in the long silk cream sherwani of the groomsmen, accompanied by a light green scarf.

"They're ready for her," the young boy said quietly and waved at Sangeeta from the door. "You look amazing."

Sangeeta smiled, willing everyone to leave as her stomach continued to roil.

"Thank you." Toral nodded and shut the door. She did a quick once-over of Sangeeta, and finding nothing but perfection, she smiled and nodded.

"Whenever you're ready." Her voice was soft and gentle, not at all bossy or demanding, but suddenly Sangeeta had the urge to tell Toral to stop telling her what to do.

Sangeeta pressed her lips together and looked back in the mirror. Her choli blouse and skirt were red with a gold border and beaded embroidery throughout. She had chosen the pattern and the cut, and had worked closely with the seamstress until satisfied. Sangeeta needed it to match her vision perfectly. Her hair was up in a braided high bun, secured with a plethora of hairpins and adorned with jasmine flowers. She'd gone simple with the bridal jewelry, letting the choli make its statement.

"You're gorgeous." Tina leaned her face next to hers and gave her a squeeze. "The perfect bride."

Sangeeta smiled her gratitude.

Anita waited by the door. "Ready?"

Sangeeta's stomach dropped again. Normal. That must be normal. "Sure."

Anita grinned and opened the door, starting down the steps. Tina followed, and Sangeeta followed behind her bridesmaids, her jhanjhar jingling softly with each step. She had opted to go barefoot down the aisle, to give her jhanjhar their moment. Toral brought up the rear.

Sweat beaded on her forehead as they approached the closed double doors on the main floor. Toral went to the doors and turned to face them, her expression tight and formal. This was a wedding, after all; things needed to be done on time and smoothly. Sangeeta respected that work ethic and considered poaching the girl for her own company, when she went out on her own. Though that would not be for four more years. Sangeeta needed to acquire more of a reputation, get some regular clients to go with her when she left Lilliana.

A hand waved in front of her. "Yoo-hoo. Earth to Sangeeta." Anita's singsong voice interrupted her thoughts.

"What are you thinking about?" Tina asked. "You better not be thinking about work as you get ready to marry a super-hot, super-sweet man." Tina eyed her with suspicion.

Sangeeta closed her eyes and inhaled. Tina was right. This was most definitely not the time to be thinking about her business. She was getting ready to walk down the aisle and take the next step in her life. She was getting married. To Param Sheth, who was indeed handsome and very kind, and smart and... She was going to spend the rest of her life with him and only him.

Just the two of them.

Which was great. Because she loved him. And he loved her.

Forever and ever.

And...ever.

She cracked her neck and felt Tina and Anita flank her on either side, just a step behind her. She did not have maternal uncles, so she had asked Tina and Anita to walk with her. Sangeeta turned her head to the right and opened her eyes.

The side door was open, allowing a gentle breeze to come in. It opened to a small Baltimore side street, but Sangeeta could see clear blue skies behind the building across the street. A cool breeze blew through the hall where she stood. It was midmorning, and it would warm up as the day progressed. Not even the weather dared to ruin Sangeeta Parikh's perfectly planned wedding day.

She looked at the double doors again and inhaled. Graduate, get a job, get married. First child in four years, then eventually two more. She'd prefer to have a girl first, but she had no real control over *that*.

But getting married at this point in her life was part of her plan. And Sangeeta *always* stuck to her plan. What were you without a plan? Chaos. And chaos was not acceptable.

Toral met her gaze. "Sangeeta?"

"It's time." Toral's voice sounded very far away.

Sangeeta turned toward Toral, focused on the girl's hand as she reached for the pull on the double doors.

Then everything seemed to happen in slow motion.

"I'm sorry, I can't." The words were out of Sangeeta's mouth before she even realized what she was saying. She turned her feet, her body and her soul toward the sun and she ran.

Chapter Two

Sonny Pandya had been at his restaurant since 6:00 a.m. that morning. He was always grateful for the morning chai and coffee crowd. It slowed down around 9:30 a.m., which allowed him to make a pot of chai for his staff to enjoy before they prepped for midmorning snack and lunch. Indian street food could be eaten anytime, so he had to be available when people wanted to eat.

Sonny sipped his midmorning chai as he and his maître d', Kamila, went over the day. His head sous chef, Dharm, tapped his fingers, impatient to get on with the day. They weren't fast food, but they weren't fancy either. They were comfortable. Sonny wanted his customers to feel safe and at home in his restaurant.

"We're good right now with one full-time and one

part-time waitstaff," Kamila said as she sipped her chai. "But the part-timer, Priya, is looking for more hours."

"I'd be happy to train her in the kitchen." Dharm placed his hands on the table and leaned in.

"What about Naya?" Sonny asked. "I thought she was great in the kitchen."

"She's getting busier with school." Dharm shook his head. "We need someone who can consistently come in and work."

Sonny finished the last of his chai and nodded. "Ask Priya if she wants to work in the kitchen as well. I'm all about people who want to work." He rinsed his mug in the sink and put it in the industrial-sized dishwasher. He grabbed the trash from the can.

"Boss. I can take that out." Dharm started to walk over.

Sonny waved him off. "Finish your chai. You still have—" he glanced at the small Ganesha-shaped clock on the wall " —six minutes before you need to start cooking again." Sonny chuckled and carried the bag through the door to the hallway that led to the alley.

The back door was slightly ajar—he'd gotten in the habit of leaving it open a crack after more than one incident of locking himself out. He was walking down the back hall, past his office with the trash bag, when he heard a small scream of pain accompanied by what could only be described as jingling. He dropped the bag and rushed to the back door.

A young woman in a very fancy red choli was clearly out of breath, muttering to herself. A bride—yes, her hair was up, complete with flowers, and she was adorned as a bride would be—had one hand against his door and was trying, unsuccessfully, to stand up.

"Whoa there." He reached for her. "Hold on. You're bleeding."

"Oh my god. Oh my god. What did I do?" She was looking at her foot as she muttered, but she reached out wildly and he grabbed her hand.

"I think you stepped on glass," he said, trying to steady her. The aroma of jasmine surrounded her. He inhaled it deeply, the sweet perfume of it somehow familiar. "Here. Let me help you." She nodded but continued looking at her foot. He helped her balance while pulling over a nearby crate for her to sit on. He knelt down, took her foot in his hands and grabbed the towel that lived on his shoulder to stop the blood.

"Wow," he said, examining the cut. "Lucky the amount of blood is not proportional to the cut."

"Well, why is there broken glass on the street?" she snapped.

"It's a back alley," he said, his own irritation building instantly. "Why are you out in an alley barefoot?" he countered.

She continued looking down at her foot.

"You're going to need more than this towel." He'd seen worse. His sister, Reena, had always been injuring herself growing up, and he'd always been the one to patch her up. He wrapped the cut with the towel. "I can fix you up quick and get you back to your wedding in time. I mean, you're clearly late." He pointed a thumb behind him at the people who had their phones up, taking video or pictures. "But you're attracting attention out here."

She looked up and past him at the onlookers, and he was instantly transported back in time. The smell of sunscreen and the sound of the ocean hit him as if it were really there.

He hadn't seen her in almost a year. She was the beach, summer cocktails and the night stars. Anger welled up inside him as he recalled the pain of his last conversation with her over the bitter taste of black coffee. She had told him she was getting engaged before she had walked away from him. "You!"

She jerked her gaze to him and her beautifully made-up eyes widened. "You!"

"What the hell are you doing here?" Gone was the kind Samaritan.

"I cut myself—didn't you see the blood?" she snapped at him as if the nine months had not passed between them.

"Do you always run around dressed like a bride?"

"I *am* a bride," she said with no small amount of indignation.

"What are you doing out here, then? With no shoes?"

"I—" She glanced behind him. "Oh crap! They're coming down the alley." She stood and teetered. He caught her arm, balancing her. She tried to take a step toward the door and cried out in pain. The phone people were getting closer. She took another step.

"Where are you going?"

"Inside, to get away from these—people." She tried another step and groaned in pain.

Sonny sighed. Sangeeta Parikh was the last person he'd ever thought he'd see again, but their paths continued painfully, to cross, as if the universe had to keep reminding him that she had chosen another man over him.

He looked behind him. Sure enough, the crowd was getting closer, like aliens in a movie, curious about the bride in the alley. Why was she in an alley?

"Fine." He bent down and picked her up like a baby.

"What the hell are you doing? Put me down!" She kicked her feet and tried to jump out of his arms.

"Do you want to get away from these people or not?" Sonny grunted at her.

"I do."

"Then stop—" he dodged her arm "—moving. I'll take you inside."

"Hey! Hey! Stop! Bride—what's your name? Why are you here?' Did you run from your wedding?" The people with their phones pointed at them were getting closer, calling out to her.

"Hurry up, then!" she commanded him as if she hadn't been the one holding them up.

"Open the door." He turned so she could reach the door, careful not to bang her head on it. But now they were both facing the crowd.

"Hey! Is this your boyfriend? Did you run from your wedding for this guy?"

"Yes," Sangeeta said. "That's what I did," she snarked at the young woman, with an eye roll worthy of even the most sullen teenager.

He heard the sarcasm in her voice and he knew there was no way it was true, but he snapped his head to look at her on reflex, as if even his body held out a molecule of hope that somehow what she said was true. It was less than a split second, but his heart crashed just the same as reality reared its head.

"No. No! That is not what— " Sonny started to explain. Sangeeta's body in his arms fit surprisingly well.

"Then why are you carrying her?"

"She's—" He looked at her a moment, realizing that for all the time they'd spent together, this was the first time he'd ever touched her. He gathered her more securely even as her shiny painted mouth curled into a frown. "Injured."

"Can we just go in?" she hissed. She was holding the door open, so Sonny stepped back and in, carefully turning so as not to bang any part of her on the doorjamb. The door closed completely behind them.

"Did you just tell them you ran away from your wedding for me?" He took a few steps toward his office.

"Don't be ridiculous." Sangeeta tried to look away from him, even as she gripped his neck tighter. "Of course I didn't."

"You kind of did."

"Sonny Pandya." She glared at him, but the sound of his name on her voice, even with the irritation it held now, was a balm to his soul that he absolutely did not want to acknowledge. "There is no way on this earth that I would run from my wedding to you."

"Yeah?" He raised an eyebrow and smirked at her as he entered his office, his arms filled with her body. "Yet here you are."

Chapter Three

"Let me down." She demanded. "Let me down, now." What the hell had just happened? Ten minutes ago she was laughing with her besties in a beautiful bridal suite. Now she was in the arms of a man who was not her husband, her foot wrapped in a dish towel, throbbing with pain. She had run, *run* from her own wedding, and ended up, of all places, with none other than Sonny Pandya.

Who was smirking at her with his perfect mouth and looking at her with eyes that nearly saw through her.

Sonny took a few large steps into what looked like a small office, and set her down on a small sofa, before accusing her. "You just told them you ran from your wedding for me."

"Don't flatter yourself."

"It's not flattery, trust me," he snapped back at her.

"I was being sarcastic. Anyone could tell that." She dismissed his concern.

"You know that. I know that. They—" he flicked a thumb in the direction of the back door "—do not know that."

She shrugged. "What difference does it make?"

Sonny let out a large sigh as he shook his head at her. "Whatever. I'll fix that up for you while you wait for someone to come get you." He handed her a card from his desk. "This is the address." He walked out before she could say anything. She had no phone on her to call anyone. She had nowhere to go. She had no choice but to let Sonny fix her throbbing foot. All she wanted was to flee this office, the way she had fled the mandap.

Though she had no idea where she would flee to. Panic strangled her heart, making it hard to breathe for a moment. She literally had nowhere to go. She inhaled and exhaled, controlling her heart rate. Her foot needed fixing first. *Small steps.*

Sonny returned shortly, his black sneakers squeaking softly. He wore chef's whites with the top buttons undone, revealing a dark T-shirt underneath, and black slacks. Sonny was tall, and if memory served her, he was quite fit underneath that jacket. He brought with him a small bowl of haldi paste and some cotton and gauze. Sonny handed her the bowl of haldi paste and knelt in front of her again, pulling her mehndi-decorated foot onto his knee. He rolled up the sleeves of his jacket, revealing the muscular forearms she had made herself forget. He removed the towel that was now stained with her blood, with a gentle touch that contrasted with his brisk demeanor.

His hand hovered over her jhanjhar. "May I?"

She hesitated a fraction of a second before nodding.

Strong, deft fingers quickly removed the belled anklet, which he held out to her. He did not do more than graze her ankle with the tips of his fingers, but his touch zinged nonetheless. She put her hand out to get the anklet, and disappointment flashed through her when he simply dropped it into her hand.

Sonny produced a warm damp washcloth to clean the area, taking his time, careful not to hurt her.

"Haldi paste?" Sangeeta asked as the musty aroma filled her nostrils, taking her back to her childhood when her grandmother used this paste on everything from cuts to bruises to broken bones.

"It's the best." A small smile broke through his smirk, brightening his features. "My grandmother used to make it whenever we had an injury. It's a bit messy, but over the years, I found that a good secure gauze wrap kept the turmeric from leaking out and staining everything." He flicked warm brown eyes up at her, her foot on his knee. "Plus, it's always in the kitchen." His voice was deep and pleasant. It took her back to the rumble of the ocean and aroma of the salty air.

"Yes. My mom still does it." She flicked her eyes to him. "Your thumb was wrapped like this. On the beach."

Sonny glanced at her, his mouth set. "Work hazard. Sharp knives." Silence built between them as Sonny went about cleaning and treating her wound. She'd never touched him when they'd met on the beach almost nine months ago. She wasn't touching him now, but one of his hands held her ankle steady as he smoothed on haldi paste with the fingers of the other. His touch was sure, each stroke achingly gentle. She tried to ignore the comfort she felt even from that small and inconsequential feathering of his skin on hers.

"Not too bad of a cut. Just the location is bad. You'll feel better in a few days. And at least it's not your driving foot." He continued to apply a generous amount of haldi paste, with practiced fingers. Then he covered it with cotton, then the gauze, so it was secure. His hands moved with such agility and confidence that Sangeeta involuntarily flushed under his touch. What was the matter with her?

"It looks like your thumb healed well." She said, trying to take her focus off of him touching her.

His gaze flicked to her. "It's fine." He gave a sharp nod as he stood. "You might limp down the aisle, but you'll be fine."

She stared at him. She was going to have to admit what she'd done. "I don't have my phone."

"You're walking around without shoes and without a phone?" He furrowed his brow. "What's going on?"

She pursed her lips, considering how much to tell him. The reality of her situation was that she needed to just tell him the truth. Or the minimum that he needed to know.

"I really did run from my wedding."

His very handsome features were a sight to behold, particularly as he processed this information. Furrowed brow, full mouth pursed, confused dark brown eyes, squarely clenched jaw. She saw the moment it hit him. His entire face changed, pulled tight in anger.

"Wait. You ran from your *wedding*. The guy who called—" Sonny pressed his lips together in a line.

"I didn't run from *Param*, I ran from my life with him."

"Same thing." Sonny was short.

"No. It's not." Sangeeta set her own jaw. There was a distinction. This was not because of Param in any way. Except that he was not the person she wanted to spend the rest of her life with. Might have been nice to have had this realization anytime earlier than today, but there it was. "Not that you need to understand. I'll just go." Sangeeta stood, putting her weight on her uninjured foot. She'd have to figure this out. She had run; it was her problem. She tried to take a step and collapsed as sharp pain shot up through her injured foot when she tried to use it. She teetered and braced herself for a fall when a strong hand grabbed her and pulled her into an arm that was quickly becoming familiar. Her heart raced, though she convinced herself it was from almost falling and not from having Sonny's arm around her again for the second time in twenty minutes.

"You might have to wait until someone comes to get you."

"No one is coming to get me." She spoke softly as the truth of that statement overcame her. Sonny guided her safely back to the sofa. As soon as he released her, she shivered, as if only he had been keeping her warm.

"What do you mean?"

"What part of 'I ran' don't you get?" she threw at him.

Sonny stayed quiet and raised an eyebrow at her.

She inhaled. "It wasn't planned. No one knows where I am. I have no phone. I can probably go back into the hotel in the back door and sneak up to my room."

"You can't walk." Sonny stated this as if it were fact. He held his phone out to her. "Call someone."

She shook her head. She did not want to take his help. He didn't move his phone. She snatched his phone from his hands as if it had offended her.

It went straight to voice mail and Sangeeta hung up. Within seconds, the phone buzzed in her hands.

"Tina."

"Oh my god! Sangeeta. Where are you? What happened? What's going on?" Tina's voice was hushed, but Sangeeta could hear people in the background.

"I'm at—" She looked at Sonny. "Where am I?" she mouthed

He rolled his eyes and shook his head. "The Masala Hut."

"I'm at The Masala Hut." She repeated to Tina.

"What the hell is The Masala Hut?"

"A restaurant, a couple blocks down from the hotel. I need a ride." She tried not to sound desperate, especially in front of Sonny, who was clearly not impressed by her breakaway. Not that running from your wedding was something impressive.

"Yeah. Okay. I can't come now. It's a zoo around here." Tina was whispering into the phone. "If anyone finds out that we've talked—oh, gotta go. Rani." Tina hung up.

Sangeeta stared at the phone for a moment. She was stuck. In a situation of her own making. This was why one always had to have a plan.

"A bit off-plan, huh?" Sonny raised an eyebrow at her.

"Of course," she snapped, but not before she registered that he had remembered how she loved a plan, just from those three days they spent at the beach. Huh. "Who would plan to run from their wedding?"

Sonny narrowed his eyes. "Who would actually run from their wedding?" he shot back.

Okay. That was enough. She wasn't going to sit here with this overly handsome chef in his sexy glasses and be judged. That's what her mother was for. She stood and suppressed her moan of pain. "Thanks for the haldi. I'll get the towel back to you." She took a step and ignored the pain that zinged her foot. She took another couple of steps. Ah. She could do this. She had no idea where she was going to go. But hiding out here—

"You might not want to keep walking—"

"I'm fine!"

"Um, I don't think so." He nodded down at her foot.

Blood was seeping through the gauze and onto the floor. Damn it!

She wanted to cry. She wanted to wail, but she had made her decision. Crying would not fix it, but she would most definitely need to swallow some pride. She looked up at him. She wasn't sure what showed on her face, besides desperation, but something softened in him.

He scrubbed his face and sighed. "Have a seat. I'll fix it."

She stood there, hating the fact that she had to sit down and let him fix her foot—again. Hating the fact that she *needed* someone. That of all people, she needed him. She inhaled and sat down without a word. Sonny kneeled again and redid her dressing with fresh haldi and gauze. He said nothing, and neither did she. Her silence allowed her to focus on his touch, how nimbly he was able to rewrap her foot. She focused on suppressing her tears instead of the fact that Sonny was touching her again.

"I… I…um, well, thank you," she started. She swallowed hard, pushing down her tears and choking down her pride. "I need to stay here if that's all right. My closest friends are… Well, they're being watched." She found it difficult to make eye contact, though she felt him watching her intently.

"Sure." He narrowed his eyes at her. "Why not? My office is your refuge. I mean, after all, you do what you want, when you want, with very little thought to anyone else."

"That is not true!" she shot at him.

He raised his eyebrows at her, firing up. "You left me at the beach, and your poor fiancé just now in the mandap."

"The beach was…different. I explained—"

He waved away her explanation. "You'll have to stay. There's no way you're going anywhere on that foot. I suppose you'll need food, too?"

Sonny shook his head and left his office. Of course he was going to feed her. Feeding people was like an instinct. He couldn't help himself. He didn't want to feed her. What he needed was for her to leave. He did not have the time or bandwidth to get involved with her. Not again.

Sonny Pandya believed in true love. He could not be Harish and Jaya Pandya's son without believing in true love. His parents' marriage might have been arranged, but truer love there had never been. His parents loved each other with respect and kindness, and Sonny would settle for no less than that for himself. He had watched them build their hotel business from the ground up, and no matter how stressful things had gotten, or how many differences of opinion they'd voiced, they had always come to each other in love. Holding hands or catching each other's eye, or in other small, affectionate ways, they held their connection to each other. He thought he might have touched on it when he spent those few days with Sangeeta at the beach.

He had started to have real feelings for her at the beach all those months ago. Feelings that were wonderful and scary all at the same time. Feelings that had happened so fast, he wasn't even sure they were real at the time. But then Param had called for a reconciliation, and it was over before it started.

He had worked these last nine months to fade those feelings as he occupied himself with building his restaurant. His sister was pushing for him to date, and he had been considering it. He had relegated those beach days to simply an odd blip in his life. Until he'd found Sangeeta bleeding outside his door thirty minutes ago.

Seeing her today brought not only the anger he'd felt when she had gone back to her fiancé, but also how he'd felt connected to her like he'd never felt with anyone. She was not good for him. She had been clearly committed to marrying this other guy—and then she ran. Sonny did not need any part of this. It had been hard enough last time.

These thoughts floated through his head as he washed the lentils and rice to make khichdi for the woman he was trying to avoid.

"Uh—Chef? What's with the small pot of khichdi?" Dharm asked.

"I found a runaway bride in the alley." Sentences one never knew they would say.

"Oh, okay." Dharm did not seem fazed by his words. Sonny found out why in his next breath.

"I saw it on Insta," Dharm continued.

"Saw what?" That was too fast. Even for social media. It had been thirty minutes, tops.

Dharm produced his phone and showed Sonny. There it was, a video of him carrying Sangeeta into the back of the restaurant. It looked like any alley. There was no audio.

"Hmph." Too bad the restaurant sign wasn't more prominent, just the faint etching of it in the back door; he could have used the publicity. He went back to his khichdi and promptly forgot about the video. "Here, keep chopping." He handed Dharm a few bunches of cilantro. "Lunch crowd incoming."

Chapter Four

Sonny left his office, leaving Sangeeta alone with only her thoughts. She inhaled and exhaled with purpose, keeping her breathing steady. She could not afford a full-blown panic attack right now. She hadn't had one in over nine months. Since Param had thought they needed to wait to get married.

Waiting had not been part of her plan. But Param had been having second thoughts. He loved her, but things were moving too fast, he'd said. He felt they needed a break.

Sangeeta had spontaneously gone to the beach to think. To be alone, away from her family, who couldn't stop fawning over her about the sudden breakup. She had found a room in a hotel on the beach and left. Sonny had found her hyperventilating on the beach, a drink in hand.

Imagine her surprise, when a week later, her mother showed her his profile from the Indian marriage site.

Her foot throbbed in pain, a true reminder of what could happen when one did things spontaneously. She tested it to see if she could stand, and when that felt tolerable, she tried to take a step. The intensity of the pain had her sitting down again. Served her right for leaving without her chappal. What was she thinking?

That was just it, wasn't it? She hadn't been thinking. She had acted on pure emotion—something she rarely—if ever—did. But standing in that hallway, waiting for Toral to open the door to the rest of her life, she had panicked. She felt suffocated, heavy, filled with dread. The feeling she'd had all morning in her stomach had not been bridal nerves, it had been dread. She had seen brides freak out in the days before their weddings, but then on their wedding day, they were fine. Some even freaked out getting ready, but they always went through with it. Maybe she should have followed up to see if they were happy.

It was as if something in her cracked open and she realized that she was getting ready to spend the rest of her life with this man with whom, she'd had to admit in that moment, she had no real connection. Param was very handsome and sweet and he was a wonderful teacher— but, if she was finally being honest, there had always been something missing.

Her parents had that spark, even after close to thirty-three years of being married. People always marveled at her parents' relationship. On the surface, it seemed that her mother ran everything, her father was simply the man who followed. And maybe it was, but Sangeeta had seen the love between them as she was growing up. It was in the way they worked at the office together, or cooked together. The way her father rubbed her mother's feet and the way she ironed his shirts. The sparkle in their eyes when they looked at each other.

Sangeeta was no fool, however; she understood that not everyone could have what her parents had. It didn't stop her from wanting it. She had so badly wanted there to be that spark with Param, but every other box was checked with him, so she figured it would come with time.

Then she had seen the sun. It had been gray and lightly raining all morning—good luck for a wedding, someone had said—but in that moment there was sun.

The next thing she knew, she was running toward it. The surprised gasps and calls of Anita and Tina had barely registered as she ran toward what could only be called freedom. She knew she was attracting attention. She even thought she might have caught a glimpse of one of Param's groomsmen from the corner of her eye. She'd only gone a few blocks before she saw the alley and cut down it. She had no idea where she was going when she'd felt a sharp, searing pain on the side of her foot. She'd crumpled, just as a door opened.

She'd had no idea it was Sonny Pandya's restaurant. Sonny, whom she'd randomly met at the beach almost a year ago. Whom her mother had set her up with a week later, when she had already returned from the beach for Param.

Param was part of the plan. Sonny Pandya was not. So then, how the hell did she end up in his office, dressed in her wedding choli, with a gash on the side of her foot, trying to steady her breathing?

With no phone and no money.

She pulled up her injured foot and laid it across her other leg. She pulled up her chaniya and started to release the knot of the small cloth that Sonny had tied on her mehndi-covered foot over the gauze.

"Don't touch that." Sonny's voice was sharp, and she startled as if she had been caught doing something wrong. Which she most certainly was not. It was her foot after all.

"The pressure. Needs to stay constant." His voice was gentler now and she turned to him. He carried a tray with a few bowls on it. The aroma made her stomach growl. He set down the tray on his desk and turned back to her. He did not make eye contact with her as he knelt in front of her. The sleeves of his whites were still rolled up. He wielded those bronzed and corded forearms with impunity.

He raised his hands to her ankle, hesitating a moment until she removed her hands. "Let's take a look." He then untied the towel and set it aside.

"Well, it's not bleeding through this gauze, which is good." His voice remained clinical, as though he were a doctor.

"Were you premed or something?" Her every thought seemed to tumble out of her mouth when she was around him.

He looked at her, eyes narrowed. "I used to tend to my brother's and sister's injuries all the time. I've known I was a chef since I was ten years old." He nodded at her foot. "That's just basic first aid." That adorable small smile poked through. "With an Indian twist." He finally made eye contact. He had the softest deep brown eyes—not black—but a legit deep brown—framed by long lashes she would have paid money for.

"Well, I was premed—"

"Of course you were." That adorable smile quickly became an irritating smirk.

"What the hell does that mean?"

"You're a rule follower. You like your plans." He stated things as if he knew her. "It makes sense that you would have stayed the expected course and been premed in college."

"There is nothing wrong with trying premed."

"Of course not. If that's what you want. Which you clearly did not since you're a wedding planner now." He paused. "So, it begs the question as to why you tried it in the first place."

He didn't know her. Except that he was right.

"Not everyone is born knowing exactly what they are destined for," Sangeeta shot back.

"Uh-huh." He acted like he was agreeing but Sangeeta had the niggling feeling he was not. Whatever. She didn't have to prove anything to him, or anyone else. "Of course, now you're a wedding planner who ran from her own wedding."

Sangeeta opened her mouth to retort, but she had nothing. "Well, at least no one knows."

He nodded and stood. "I need to get back to the kitchen." He gestured toward the tray. "Help yourself."

She eyed the tray on his desk. The aromas had been taunting her since he'd entered with it. She had been fasting and she suddenly realized that she was, in fact, very hungry. "Thank you." She tried to put as much formality in her voice as possible. They hardly knew each other. And she had no desire to hang out here any longer than necessary.

"Of course," he mumbled as he left.

She managed to hobble the few steps to the desk and sat down in the chair, finding it surprisingly comfortable. There was a steaming bowl of khichdi in the middle with a rolled cloth napkin and silverware. There was a small clay pot of ghee, another with yogurt and a few more with varying hot or sweet pickles. A thin round disc of crispy papad was balanced on the edge of her bowl. The khichdi was soul nourishing, along with the crisp and spicy papad.

She mixed in the ghee and then smoothed over the top, gently spreading the spicy pickle over it, then crumbling the papad over the top. Normally, she would have eaten with her hands, because that was true comfort, but she had a lot of jewelry on her hands at the moment, so she used the spoon.

The khichdi was the perfect consistency, the tang from the pickle and the crunch from the papad combined to make her feel warm and content. For a split second, she was back in India, in her grandmother's kitchen with all her cousins. For a few moments, nothing else existed except this wonderful food.

She became aware of being watched. She looked up and found Sonny looking at her.

"What? I thought you were in the kitchen."

"I was. I—" He cleared his throat. "I've never seen someone react to my food—that way."

"What do you mean?" She kept a steady flow of food

into her mouth, never wanting it to end. "Eating it?" she snarked. What? He set it up.

"No." He grimaced at her. "You, ah. Well." He pressed his lips together. "You moaned."

"I most certainly did not." Did she?

He side-smiled, and her insides became the same consistency as the khichdi. "You absolutely did."

Well, that was embarrassing. She shrugged it off as if it meant nothing even as she felt heat rise to her face. "Well, I've been fasting. This is food."

His face hardened. "Whatever." He crossed the small space and opened the door to what Sangeeta could see was a cluttered storage area. He walked into it and emerged in a couple of minutes with a package of plates and plasticware. Sangeeta kept shoveling his amazing khichdi into her mouth. He glanced at her, a small smirk coming over his lips. The sound of a phone buzzing stopped him.

He fished his phone out of his pants pocket. Sangeeta noted that his sleeves were still rolled up. She shook her head. What the hell was wrong with her? She was literally about to marry someone else this morning, and here she was lusting after this chef's forearms. She did an internal eye roll. Good thing she ran.

"Hello?" He nodded, a frown coming over his face. He walked over to her and handed her the phone. "It's for you. I'll be back for the phone."

She downed the lassi before taking the phone. So cool and tart and refreshing. "Hello."

"Sangeeta." Tina was whispering into the phone. "I cannot come. Rani is eyeing me. Anita is busy handling food and your mom is—"

"Ballistic."

"Pretty much." Tina sighed. "I'll see what I can do. How long can you hang out at that place?"

"I don't know." She eyed where Sonny had stood. This was really the last place she wanted to be. At least he was not going to want to keep her any longer than she wanted. "I don't even have a change of clothes."

"Let me figure something out."

"Thanks, Tina. You're the best." Sangeeta ended the call and returned to her food. All that was left was for her to lick the bowl, which she was contemplating when something on his desk caught her eye. Next to his cardholder was a small, dried starfish. Her heart did a thud. He had actually kept this? She reached out to touch it, just as a woman bounded into the office. Sangeeta snapped her hand away from the starfish.

The woman was in workout clothes and was slightly out of breath. Even though she looked like she had just run from wherever she had been and was dripping sweat, she was gorgeous. The woman stopped and a sly grin came across her face.

"We've been telling my brother to get married, but I didn't expect him to have a bride just sitting in his office."

"Oh. I'm not a bride. I mean I am a bride, but I'm not his bride. I'm not even a bride." Not anymore.

The woman raised an eyebrow, clearly amused.

"It's complicated." Sangeeta sighed.

"I can see that." She smiled and extended her hand. "Reena Pandya. Sonny's sister."

"Sangeeta Parikh. I—that's all I have."

"Runaway bride?" Her smirk was similar to her brother's, but significantly much less irritating.

"Yes. That's it." Sangeeta smiled, and a giggle escaped, despite the obvious gravity of the situation. That's who she was right now. Runaway Bride.

"Do I even want to know?" Reena raised an eyebrow.

"I ended up in the alley, cut my foot. Sonny found me bleeding."

"And he fixed you up." She nodded at the tray, which was now clean of food. "And fed you." Reena chuckled and shook her head. "That's my brother. He fixes everything." There was love and pride in her voice that touched Sangeeta.

Sonny returned to the office and stopped when he saw his sister. "Reena. Hey. What's up?"

"Just came to see to my big brother, and I see you are harboring runaway brides."

Sonny rolled his eyes and shook his head, but there was something light and playful about the interaction that made Sangeeta smile. He turned to her. "Got a ride coming?" he sounded eager for her to leave.

"No. Everyone is—" She cut her eyes to Reena. "Busy."

She wiggled a bit in the chair.

"Itchy clothes?" Reena nodded at her.

"Yes. No matter what material, something always itches."

"I know, right? I keep a few things at Sonny's apartment. You are welcome to borrow if you want," Reena offered.

The idea was tempting. The choli was not only itchy, it was getting stifling. She tried not to think of the significance of that. Her head hurt from all the pins keeping her hair up. If she wasn't getting married, it seemed pointless to be so uncomfortable.

"He lives over the restaurant," Reena continued.

"That actually sounds amazing, but I have imposed enough—"

Reena waved a hand. "You stick out right now—all your people are looking for a bride. Think of it as expediting your release from here. Believe me, I can totally understand wanting to get out of here."

"I'm standing right here, baby sister. I can hear you," Sonny mumbled.

"Good." Reena laughed. "Come on." She waved Sangeeta to follow her.

Sangeeta stood and took a step, testing her foot out. She was able to put pressure on her big toe and hobble along slowly. Satisfied, she followed Reena out of the office to a set of stairs she had not noticed before. She proceeded slowly up the stairs behind Sonny's sister. She reached the landing and followed Reena into the small apartment. Reena bustled in and to the bedroom.

Sangeeta took a moment to see where Sonny Pandya lived. She was currently standing just inside the door, and the open kitchen area to her left took up most of that side. A breakfast bar ran the length of the kitchen, a small table with two chairs on the far end by a window that overlooked the street. To her right was a small living area with a sofa, a table and a small TV. One bedroom, which she glimpsed when Reena had entered.

Reena produced leggings and a T-shirt and handed them to Sangeeta. "I keep these here in case I sleep over."

"Thank you." Sangeeta looked at the clothes like

they were the source of her freedom. She found the bathroom and quickly took off her choli, donning the leggings and T-shirt. The leggings stretched to fit. The T-shirt was a bit snug, but better than the choli. She felt like a new person. Her hair still hurt, but it was better.

"See, you're immediately more relaxed." Reena glanced at her watch. "Can you make it down? I have a meeting and I still need to run back and shower."

Sangeeta nodded. "Sure."

She limped her way down the steps and back into Sonny's office. He was at the now-cleared-up desk on his computer. She limped to the sofa and sat down. She considered asking about the starfish, but then thought better of it. She slowly started removing bobby pins from her hair, making a pile of them. She took in her surroundings. Labeled boxes of supplies were piled up haphazardly across the space. The door to the storage area was open, and Sangeeta immediately began mentally arranging the boxes in it. "You could easily fit all this in that area," she said.

"I need to be able to access everything easily," he said, without looking at her.

"You could. It's all in how you place it and making easily readable labels."

"It's fine how it is."

She shrugged. "It's your mess."

"That it is."

She continued removing pins until she couldn't anymore. A few remained. She could feel them but couldn't reach them.

"Need help with the pins?"

"No. I'm fine."

"My sister used to dance. I had to always get those pins out."

"I'm fine."

He shrugged. "Suit yourself."

His phone buzzed. He glanced at it and handed it to her.

Tina had texted. Rani followed me to the bathroom. I cannot leave.

She glanced at the kitchen utensil clock in the room. It had been a few hours since she ran. She started to face the idea that she was quite literally stuck. She couldn't limp around town in bare feet. And even if she could, where would she go? Param was staked out at the apartment. Her mother was at the hotel. Everyone was waiting for her to reveal where she was. She couldn't just sit here. She stood.

"No one knows where I am except for Tina. Your sister was right. I don't stand out now, so I can move about if I want." Sangeeta inhaled and closed her eyes. She hated asking for help, but she could not very well sit here all day. "If you call me an Uber, I'll Venmo you back."

"Where will you go?"

"That is not your concern. You have been kind enough to help with my foot."

"You don't know where you can go." He pushed up his glasses as he looked at her.

She simply held up her head and said nothing.

"Okay." He stood and walked over to her. "Sit down. You look ridiculous with those pins stuck in your hair. I'll get those last ones out while you think. Then I'll call you an Uber. You can go your way, I'll go mine."

"Fine."

"Fine."

She sat back down. Sonny came up behind her. His touch was as gentle as it had been when he tended to her foot. She barely felt the pins come out. It was quite soothing, and she closed her eyes and relaxed for the first time all day, her body going limp. She might have been drifting off to sleep when she became aware of voices and a commotion nearby. Familiar voices. Coming from the front of the restaurant.

"I know she's here. The restaurant name is in the video."

Param.

What video? How had he found her? Before she could process, he was in the office. She stood, just as Sonny pulled the last pin from her hair, and the last strands tumbled down around her face and below her shoulders.

"Sangeeta! What are you—" He looked at Sonny, who had his hands in her hair. He took a step toward Sonny, anger oozing from him. "What the hell are you doing with your hands in my fiancée's hair?"

Sonny did not flinch or stop what he was doing. In fact, he showed no sign that anything had happened. "She had pins stuck in her hair."

"That's my fiancée!" barked Param. He looked awful. He was still dressed in his dream sherwani, though the top buttons were undone, he didn't have the scarf and he had put on sneakers instead of the slippers that matched. His beautiful thick hair was tousled, and he had a crazed look about him, which, in a man his size, was more than a little bit intimidating.

His eyes widened as he took her in, flicking his gaze over her, and behind her. "Param." She didn't know what else to say. Everything that came to her mind— "I'm sorry." "It's not you."—seemed lame and inconsequential.

"Sangeeta." He softened on her name and her heart broke. She was hurting him. "What's happening here? I was in the mandap, both of our parents were there—and then the doors opened, but you didn't come." His gentle soothing voice cracked. "Is this—is he why you left?"

"No. It's not like that. I hurt my foot." She lifted her foot to him. "I cut myself. There was blood everywhere. Sonny fixed it up."

Param grunted as he moved into the room. The office seemed all the smaller with Param in it, and anger simply rippled off him as he took in the space. He was looking everywhere but at her.

"Param. I—I'm sorry."

She felt Sonny retreat away from her. "I have customers," he mumbled and left her alone with Param.

Param shook his head. "Why—why—did you—run?" His voice cracked on the last word, and it broke her heart. She had broken his heart. Param was basically a big teddy bear. He had a heart of gold, and she had managed to crumble it. To make it worse, she had no explanation.

"It wasn't you," she said.

"Seriously, you're going to give me the 'it's not you, it's me' speech? You're the one who wanted to get married."

"I was wrong. I wasn't ready."

"You think?" Param ran his fingers through his hair

and looked around him. "What the—okay, whatever. Come home, Sangeeta."

"I can't."

"Come home and we can talk about this." He was almost pleading now.

"There's nothing to talk about, Param." Her voice cracked, but she remained firm.

"So, it's over, just like that?"

"Yes." He deserved whatever truthful answers she had, no matter how painful.

He closed his eyes and shook his head. "Unbelievable." He opened his eyes, his gaze landing on her as his broad shoulders sagged. "So, do you just not want to be married, or do you just not want to marry me?"

The pain in his eyes cut straight through her. She couldn't answer him.

He nodded, mouth pursed, eyes wet. "I'll get my stuff out tonight. You can go home." He swept his gaze over the cluttered office, but she knew he didn't really see anything.

She shook her head. "No. It was your apartment. I'll move out."

"Don't be ridiculous. I'll move out." He sighed. "Where would you go anyway?"

"That's not your problem, Param." Rani's voice cut through the air, sharp as a blade as she calmly entered the office. She must have been waiting outside for him. Of course she was here. Rani and Param were childhood friends –best friends, in fact. "She's the one who cut out."

Param turned his head slightly in Rani's direction. "Rani." His voice held warning.

"She's right, Param," Sangeeta said.

Over Param's shoulder, Sangeeta saw Rani cock an eyebrow at her. They had almost never agreed on anything. But today, they did. "I'll grab some stuff. I can go to Tina's." She was lying. They both knew it. All the family homes were filled with people in town for the wedding. They would not be leaving until at least tomorrow. She shrugged. "I'll figure something out."

"Sangeeta. That is not necessary."

A glance at his face and at Rani's told Sangeeta that it absolutely was. She needed to set him free if she didn't want him. She had no idea what she did want, but she'd made it clear today that she didn't want him. She couldn't just keep him dangling.

"Listen to her, Param." Rani continued to talk to his back. There was a gentleness in her voice that Sangeeta had never heard before. Or maybe she had, and she ignored it.

"Fine." He shook his head and dropped his hand, as if the fight in him was gone. "Have it your way." Rani laid her hand on his shoulder and escorted him out.

Sangeeta just stood there, staring at the closed door.

Chapter Five

Sonny had finished dinner service and he and his staff were just now going over the following day's menu, cleaning and prepping. Sangeeta was still in his office. After Param's arrival, all thoughts of getting an Uber and going somewhere seemed to have left her mind.

Though where would she go, injured and with no money? Or shoes.

"Chef? Chef? Sonny." Dharm raised his voice. "You with us?"

"Yes. I'm here."

The staff watched him, expectantly.

Dharm shook his head at him. "How about that khichdi tomorrow?" Dharm asked. "It smelled great today. You should have made more than just the one pot." He smirked.

Sonny pretended he didn't notice the smirk. "Let's add it. In fact, khichdi is such a comfort food, we should see how it does and add it permanently." They focused on street food, but comfort food could be a great complement.

They finalized the menu for the next day, and went over staffing and what had gone well today. The staff had little smiles on their faces, each of them curious about the woman in his office.

"Fine. There's a runaway bride in my office. I'm just helping her out," Sonny offered.

"Uh-huh. No one does that," Dharm said. "Not without a reason."

"My brother does, and you all know it." Reena entered the kitchen. She was stopping by again? Twice in one day. Huh. "He's just a big softie."

The entire staff nodded in agreement. Whatever. Sonny shook his head. "Go home, be with your friends and family. See you in the morning." He waved them off.

He busied himself organizing his fridge while Reena stood there. She was here for information on Sangeeta. Reena was his confidante, but she would be getting nothing today. He had confided in her his feelings all those months ago when Sangeeta had rejected him. At the time, he'd been pretty miserable, which had been irritating, because he and Sangeeta had not actually gone out.

Reena was just a couple of inches shorter than him. Her hair was pulled up in a sleek ponytail, and she wore a lime green pantsuit and heels. It was the end of the day, and to anyone else, she would appear fresh and put together. Only Sonny saw the stress in her eyes, and the set of her mouth. Her jacket carried the emblem of their parents' hotel. Reena all but ran the place.

"Hey, little sister."

"Hey."

"What brings you around?" Though he already knew. "Again?"

She shrugged. "This and that." She took a few steps closer to him and leaned against the stainless steel counter. "I heard you made khichdi today."

"It's a restaurant," he said from the fridge.

Reena narrowed her eyes at him. "I didn't know it was on the menu."

He shrugged. "It is now. You want some?"

"Yes, please." She sighed.

His sister was tired, and she needed a friend. "What?" he asked, as he gathered all the condiments on a tray, warming the khichdi in the microwave.

She shrugged. "Work."

The microwave dinged and he gathered the tray and two bowls. "Come." He led them out to a table and they sat. She started serving herself. Sonny watched her closely. She had bags under her eyes that she was trying to hide with makeup. Her lips were dry and her eyes were slightly bloodshot. His sister was seriously stressed.

"I just heard that Asha Gupta, the influencer, is having trouble with The Posh Hotel. They are unable to accommodate some of her requirements for her wedding."

"Who is Asha Gupta?"

"Seriously, big brother? She's an upcoming South Asian influencer. She has over five hundred thousand followers. She added one hundred thousand in the last few months while she's been planning her wedding."

"When's her wedding?"

"Two months."

"Well, I guess she's stuck, then. It's not like she can reschedule her wedding at this point," Sonny commented.

Reena just stared at him as she expertly put some khichdi in her mouth with her fingers.

"Unless she can?"

Reena grinned, revealing perfectly straight white teeth. "I have a proposal all ready for her if she ditches The Posh. Business has been lagging, and Asha Gupta's wedding at Lulu's Boutique Hotel would not only help financially, but we'd be in a position to be contenders again."

"Well, good luck with that." Sonny was also adept at eating khichdi with his hands. He and his siblings agreed it was the only way to eat khichdi, as taught to them by their grandmother. Their parents simply shot looks of disapproval at them, while they used spoons.

"Sonny, this is amazing. Better than Mom's." She grinned at him. "What's going on here?"

Sonny frowned and shook his head. "Not much."

"Is the bride still here?"

Sonny nodded. Sangeeta had remained holed up in his office, unable to really walk. He had brought her a tray of pav bhaji in the evening. Her eyes had widened with anticipation as he placed the tray of grilled bread with spiced potato and vegetable hash topped with butter, chopped onions and cilantro in front of her. She had eagerly torn off a piece of the bread and dipped it into the thick bhaji. When she placed the morsel in her mouth, she had closed her eyes and groaned in pleasure. Sonny had been frozen to the spot. Watching Sangeeta eat – his food– was almost sensual and intimate, in a way he'd never seen before. He'd had to leave the office.

Reena raised an eyebrow at him.

"She has nowhere to go."

"Not your problem, Bhaiya."

"It is if she's sitting in my office," Sonny countered.

Reena shook her head. "Honestly, Sonny, it amazes me that you don't have an apartment full of stray dogs."

"I would, except I have no time for them, and the health department would not approve." He chuckled. It was the truth. "What do you want?"

"Nothing. I came to check on you."

"I'm the older one. I should be doing the checking."

"So do it," she snarked.

He rolled his eyes at her. "I was just there."

"It's been two weeks."

He dutifully went to family dinner every other Sunday. His cousins and aunts and uncles came as well. They had been doing this for years. And even though it meant discomfort with his parents, he went because he loved his family. "So, I'll be there tomorrow."

"You can come at other times too, you know," she said softly.

"Reena…"

She held up her hands in surrender. "I know. I know. You're mad at Mom and Dad."

"It's not that I'm mad at Mom and Dad, it's that they don't trust my judgment."

"I'm not getting in the middle of all that, Sonny. All

I'm saying is Jai and I miss you at home. We're used to having you around." She leaned in. "I think Jai has a girlfriend."

Sonny's heart ached for his siblings. He had practically raised them while their parents were earning a living, building up the hotel to the reputation it had today. Truth was, he missed them too. He was avoiding his parents.

"What's-his-name, the ridiculous chef. He quit." She sat and waited for this news to sink in.

Sonny froze. "Kiren? Quit?"

"Yep," she said around a mouthful of khichdi.

Silence floated between them, during which Sonny ignored his food, but Reena kept eating.

"You know how to cook the fancy food. It's guaranteed income," she finally said when her bowl had been all but licked clean.

"Did Papa send you to offer me the job?" Sonny looked up at her from under his lashes.

"I am offering you the job." Reena pushed aside her empty bowls.

"The hotel is not yours."

"Not yet." She smirked. "Give it time."

Sonny sighed. "I have a job."

"Not the same." Reena used the wipe that Sonny had left for her hands, then stood. "Amazing food as always. Thanks for feeding me." She walked toward the back.

"Say hi to Jai for me. And find out who the girl is," Sonny called.

"Say hi to him yourself. And do your own investigating."

Reena was a hard-ass, but she would pass along the

message to their younger brother. Sonny simultaneously loved and dreaded Sunday family dinner. He missed Jai and Reena, but every time he went over, he was reminded of how his father had betrayed him by not trusting his judgment.

"I'll see him tomorrow night at dinner," Sonny said to his sister's back. She paused at the door at his acceptance and waved as she left. She would put in another few hours before she turned in.

Sonny was the oldest at nearly eleven when they had come over from India. Reena was seven, and Jai was three. His parents had initially taken jobs in a motel, so Sonny and his siblings were never far from their parents. Sonny would make his siblings a snack and keep them occupied, while their mother cleaned rooms and their father ran the front. They lived frugally and worked hard so it was only a matter of time before his parents owned their own motel. They purchased one and fixed it up together. They sold it and bought a bigger one, and did the same. This had been their plan, and they made it happen.

Both of his parents came to lean on Sonny to take care of things at home. Mostly things like feeding everyone and homework. One of them managed to be home by dinnertime each day. Though by that time, Sonny had usually made dinner and fed his siblings. They praised his cooking and his sense of responsibility, so Sonny fell right into that role of surrogate parent, and maintained it moving forward.

By the time he was eighteen and attended the Culinary Institute, his parents had started Lulu's Boutique Hotel. He lived at home and continued caring for his siblings, while his parents built up the hotel. By the time Reena started college, they had two hotels, and Reena was all about getting a business degree so she could eventually run them. His parents were pleased. Reena would run the hotels, and Sonny would run the restaurants.

It had seemed a great plan. Pandya Hotels would grow as the family did. The second hotel was much smaller and in a different part of the city. They wanted a more intimate vibe. Reena ran the second hotel, but within a year, his father had been forced to sell. It hadn't been Reena's fault, but ever since then, she had become relentless in her determination to keep Lulu's in the family.

It had been a great plan, but the second hotel had simply been using up too many resources, they simply had not been ready for it.

Unfortunately, plans did not always go as expected.

Chapter Six

It was now close to nine hours since Sangeeta had bolted. She was still reeling from her conversation with Param. She should have told him how she felt sooner. Trouble was that she hadn't known until she was about to marry him.

She was sure her mother would show up at any moment. Sangeeta wanted to Uber out like she had planned, but where would she really go? She held out hope that Tina would come.

They would have been in the middle of their wedding reception right now. They would have been taking some table pictures, and dancing.

Restless, she limped around the small office. By now, she knew exactly where each box needed to be for maximum efficiency and minimum clutter. If not for her foot and Sonny's scowl each time she mentioned it, she would have made the changes by now. It was something to think about besides the awful thing she had done today.

A few photos on his desk revealed that he might also have a younger brother. She tried not to dwell too long on the fact that the starfish was on the desk as well. Suddenly overcome with fatigue, she lay down on the sofa. She closed her eyes and tried to calm her mind.

She must have slept because she was awakened by loud footsteps in heels.

"Sangeeta."

It was Tina. Thank god. She could leave.

Sangeeta sat up as her cousin entered the office. Tina was standing there in a comfy summer dress, all signs that she had been ready to attend a wedding gone. Unspent sobs built up inside Sangeeta at the sight of her best friend and cousin. She collapsed into Tina's arms.

"Hey. It's okay." Tina held her tight and Sangeeta let her tears flow. "It'll be okay."

She shook her head in Tina's arms. "No. I was horrible to him. I shouldn't have done this."

"Are you saying you want to go back to him?"

Sangeeta snapped her head up. "No. I don't want to marry Param. I just don't know what I want. And people got hurt. Good people. Because of me." She paused and wiped her face. "People got hurt because I had to stick to my stupid plan. My plan was wrong." She paused as realization hit her. "What if all my plans are wrong? What if even having a plan is wrong?"

She was blubbering and could not stop. "I mean what am I supposed to do now? I've been hiding out all day. My mom will find me. Then what? All that money we spent? My parents will be furious. Not to mention I don't even know where to go from here! What to do with my life!"

Tina was staring and nodding at her as she limp-paced in Sonny's office. "Sangeeta." She spoke softly as if afraid that normal tones might spook her. "Let's start with, where are you going to sleep tonight?"

"I was going to try your place. Or Anita's?"

Tina shook her head. "Filled with wedding guests on all accounts."

"My brother?"

Tina shook her head. "Your mom is there."

"I've been in this room for ten hours. Did you happen to bring my wallet and phone?"

Tina nodded and handed them to her. The little red circles on her notifications were in the high double dig-its. Her texts were in triple digits. She ignored them. "Perfect. Can you drive me to a hotel? I'll sleep there and figure things out in the morning."

"Or you could stay here." Sonny's sister was in the doorway.

"Hi, Reena. This is my cousin Tina." The women nodded at each other, everyone aware that decisions needed to be made. "Why would I do that?"

"Well, no one has found you yet." Reena shrugged.

"My fiancé did." *Ex-fiancé.*

"Well, yes. But no one is going to look for you in the middle of the night. And in the morning, they will assume you are with family or at a hotel. They won't think you are still here. Besides, you can hardly walk."

Sangeeta stared at the woman. She made sense. Except for one thing. "Your brother does not want me here."

Reena waved a hand. "My brother is the king of taking in strays. Last month he fostered a cat for a week. And he's allergic. Not that you're a stray cat, but you know what I mean."

Sangeeta furrowed her brow. That did not seem like the surly sarcastic man she'd seen here today. But then, how well did she know Sonny anyway? A few days at the beach wasn't everything.

"It would be weird," Sangeeta said, making eye contact with Tina.

Tina stared at her. "Seriously? After today, you're worried about weird?" she said. "Sleep on the man's couch for one night."

Sangeeta stared at her, widening her eyes, willing Tina to read her mind.

"What?" Tina demanded.

Reena grinned. "I think she's trying to tell you that Sonny is the guy she met last summer."

"You know?"

"You know?"

Sangeeta spoke at the same time as Sonny, who had just entered his office. Reena giggled. "Duh, Sonny. I read you like a book. And I never forget a name."

Tina just gaped at Sangeeta. "You kept that quiet."

"Well, it makes no difference, anyway," Sonny said, with that irritating smirk on his face. "You can have my sofa for one night, since my sister offered. Your presence in my house does not affect me. Now if *you're* uncomfortable, I'm sure my sister can put you up at Lulu's for free." He narrowed his eyes at her.

"I'm fine," Sangeeta blurted out. "I have no problem sharing space with you. Your sofa will be just fine."

"So it's settled, then," Reena said, not even trying to hide her triumph. "Sangeeta can sleep on Sonny's couch tonight."

"We'll deal with everything else tomorrow." Tina handed Sangeeta an oversized purse. "Your stuff is in there."

Sangeeta hadn't done anything spontaneous since she had gone to the beach last summer to escape her family. Having a plan meant success, it meant predictability, it meant knowing what would happen next, no surprises. It meant complete control. She liked being in control of her own life.

Her phone rang. Her mother. Crap. The absolute last person she wanted to talk to right now. Sangeeta let it go to voice mail. "Well, I don't have much choice."

"There's a lot of that going around." Sonny waved a hand in front of him.

"I'll see you tomorrow." Tina hugged her. "Good luck."

"Good night, brother." Reena waved and left.

Sonny stared at her for a moment, before leading her back to the stairs to his apartment.

Sangeeta grabbed the rail as she had when she went up earlier with Reena.

"Here." Sonny offered his arm for her to lean on.

"I'm good." No way was she taking his arm. No matter how badly she was tempted to touch him again. She'd get up the stairs on her own.

He furrowed his brow and shrugged. "Suit yourself."

It was slow going, but Sonny walked right next to her. They were silent—she could not think of anything to say—so she could hear him breathing next to her.

She imagined she could feel him touch her, but there was a good six inches between them. She took the steps like a toddler and tried not to think about the fact they were now alone, and would be spending the night under the same roof. When she reached the top, he reached around her and opened the door to let her in. "You can take the bed."

"I'll be fine on the sofa, thank you."

"Don't be ridiculous." He nearly scoffed.

"I'm not. You and I allowed ourselves to be baited into me staying here. This ridiculous situation is something I did to myself. You're...stuck in the middle. I am not kicking you out of your bed. I'll sleep on the sofa and I'll be out of your life in the morning. My foot feels better."

"Let's change that dressing." He motioned to the sofa. "Then I'll get you some sheets and a pillow."

"Okay." She considered it a win for her since her dressing needed to be changed by him regardless of where she slept. She sat on the sofa while Sonny kneeled and changed the dressing, adding more haldi paste. He had a pleasant amount of scruff on his chin and his thick hair was tousled from the day. He smelled of spices. She inhaled deeply. She was fast getting used to his gentle touch, not to mention him kneeling in front of her like this. What? She shook the errant thought from her head.

"This is healing nicely," he said.

She sat up straight, as if she had been caught doing something wrong. What was the matter with her? Or maybe the bigger question was why did he smell so good? "Haldi paste is like magic."

He chuckled. "It really is. I used it so many times

on Reena and Jai, our younger brother. Worked like a charm every time."

He finished and stood, then brought her sheets and a pillow as promised. They made up the sofa for her together.

"What are you going to do now?" he asked.

"I have no idea." Though hiding out in this room and letting her phone die sounded fabulous right now. "I guess I'll try to sleep."

He nodded. "Good night."

"Good night."

Her phone rang. Tina. She tapped the green button.

"Want to talk about it?"

"No. Yes." Sangeeta paused. She didn't even know what to say. "No. I'm just going to try to sleep."

"Sure. I'll see you tomorrow."

Sangeeta tapped the phone off as Sonny retreated to his room. She limped to the bathroom and brushed her teeth. Tina had brought her basic necessities. She went to the kitchen for water and took in her surroundings. Sparse decor. The small table was pushed up against the window. A few shelves in the small cubby space next to the table held cooking books. She looked closely at the titles, hoping to find a work of fiction she could read before she went to bed. Nothing.

She peeked out the window, catching a glimpse of the cloudless sky. Pinpoints of light greeted her. She thought of small dried starfish.

They had been walking along the beach and Sonny had suddenly cried out and started hopping around. He had stepped on something. He was uninjured, so they examined what they had found. They noted two small dried starfish. Sonny had picked them up and handed one to her. "Stars in the sky and on the beach."

She returned to the sofa and lay down. Sleep would not come. For the first time since she was eight years old, she had no idea what she was doing tomorrow.

Chapter Seven

Sonny woke to the sound of his phone buzzing. Only one person called at this hour. He had just finally found sleep in the wee hours of the morning, after tossing and turning for the better part of the night. He was exhausted, and sleep would not come. He was barraged with images from his days on the beach with Sangeeta. Images he had repressed months ago, were now returning to haunt him again.

The buzzing stopped and he tried to relax. He opened one eye to catch the time. He had to be up in five minutes. He closed his eyes. The buzzing started again.

Reena!

He could turn off his phone and pretend he never heard it buzz.

Instead, he picked up the phone and tapped it open and grunted.

"Have you seen it?" she demanded. For 5:55 a.m., she was entirely too awake, too loud and too demanding.

"Seen what?" he grumbled.

"The video," she said as if it were obvious which video she was talking about.

"Reena, it's—" he glanced at the clock "—5:59 a.m. Make sense or I hang up."

A ding came through his phone. "I just sent you a link. Open it. *Now.*"

He sighed. Fine. He put her on speaker and opened the link she sent. It was a video of a woman in a red choli, running. Then it cut to the woman in an alley, falling. He kept watching as he saw himself come out of a door and talk to the woman, before picking her up. But that wasn't the end of it. People were asking her questions.

"Hey! Is this your boyfriend? Did you run from your wedding for this guy?"

"Yes," Sangeeta said. *"That's what I did."*

Her sarcasm was clear to him, but what came next was not. The video zoomed into his face. He was looking at Sangeeta. He was looking at her like she *had* run from her wedding for him. Give the person who recorded this an Oscar for filming. They caught his split second of hope.

Denial. The best defense. "Okay, so someone has a video of Sangeeta getting injured outside in my alley. I helped her. It's all good."

"You know, Sonny, for someone so smart, you can be really dense," Reena reprimanded. "Take a look at the caption. At the number of views."

Runaway Bride ran for true love. The number of views topped one hundred thousand.

"The comments. Read the comments." Reena's voice goaded him.

Sonny skimmed the comments, and his eyes widened. They knew Sangeeta was a wedding planner. A wedding planner who had run from her own wedding. He sat up in bed. Reena was saying something about influencers and weddings, but Sonny hung up on her.

He brushed his teeth and went to wake Sangeeta. She was already up and staring at her phone, a look of shock and anger on her face. "Sangeeta. Are you okay?"

"My assistant, Toral. She just texted." Sangeeta looked up at him. Her voice was breathless, as if she'd just run a race. "There's a video."

He nodded.

"I'm the wedding planner who ran from her own wedding, and there's *video*." She looked around. She looked up at him and shook her head. "That's how Param found me. The name—The Masala Hut—it's on your back door. Did you see?"

He nodded.

Just then her phone rang. "My boss." She tapped it and put the phone to her ear. And she transformed.

"Hey, Lilliana!" Sangeeta sounded as bright and chipper as a spring bird. She nodded as her boss spoke.

Sonny stood frozen.

"Well, of course I did see—well, yes. It is true. I did. But, well, that's the interpretation. I certainly am not *with* him… Well, I'm working that out. But let me assure you that I am perfectly capable of doing my job. In fact, I am not going on my honeymoon, so I can work this week. Well, no I don't need time off... I'd prefer to work... Well, of course, Lilliana. If you think it's best."

She hung up and looked at him. "I'm going to lose my job."

Before he could say anything, the bell rang, indicating someone was at the back door. It was 6:30 a.m. Didn't anyone sleep? "Hold on." He slipped on his chappal on the way down. He opened the door to early morning sunlight and Reena in workout gear.

"Did you even hear what I said?" she asked as she made her way up the stairs. "Is she still here? Please tell me she's still here." Reena was vibrating with excitement.

"Yes, she's still here. Her boss called. Doesn't look good."

Reena froze outside his door and her eyes flicked about as she considered this. A huge smile came over her face. "That's perfect."

"What? Reena!"

Reena barged in without another word. Sangeeta was right where he'd left her, her expression blank. "Hey." Reena approached Sangeeta carefully. "I saw the video."

Sangeeta looked up, confusion all over her face, as if she was trying to process the whirlwind in front of her. "I left my fiancé alone in the mandap. I have no apartment. I'm hiding from my family. And now. Now I have no job." She turned and slowly looked at Reena as if seeing her for the first time. "Twenty-four hours ago, I had everything. Now I have nothing. All because I did not want to marry the wrong man for the wrong the reasons."

"That was smart of you. And very brave," Reena

said quietly. She motioned to Sonny to make chai. He filled a pot with water. "You are the wedding-planner-runaway-bride."

She nodded slowly. "It's absolutely ridiculous." Her eyes were glazed over as if she were still unbelieving, her usually chipper voice devoid of all emotion. Sonny found it unnerving.

"How about we have some chai and then we can talk a bit?" Reena asked.

Sangeeta nodded and headed for the bathroom. Sonny added the tea leaves and masala to the simmering water.

"Everyone can see how you looked at her in that video," Reena said quietly. "Even if she—" she pointed her thumb in the direction of the bathroom "—can't."

"I don't know what you're talking about." He focused on the chai, shredding some ginger into the pot. The ginger was fresh and sharp, and the strong scent awakened him a bit more.

"The comments are based on that look, Sonny. You *like* her. You told me you were over her, that a couple days meant nothing, but you have feelings for her," Reena pushed.

He busied himself with getting the milk from the fridge.

"Sonny!"

"Reena. What you see in that video is…is a fleeting thought. Nothing more. Trust me. I do not have feelings for Sangeeta Parikh." *That's right. Keep saying it, and it'll eventually be true.* "I mean, how could I? We spent like three days together, and never even held hands. And then as soon as her fiancé called her, she left. I have barely thought about her, nor had I seen her since. Until she showed up at my back door yesterday."

"You said you saw her at Amar Virani's Diwali party last year."

"For like two minutes. And we didn't talk." The chai was at a rolling boil. He turned it down to simmer and added a bit of sugar. He grabbed three mugs. "She announced her engagement that night. And I put her in the past." It had been harder to do than one would have imagined. For a woman whose hand he hadn't even touched.

"Sonny—"

"Let it go, Reena," he warned his sister. No good would come from him having feelings for Sangeeta Parikh.

Sangeeta emerged from the bathroom looking a bit fresher, as he poured the three mugs of chai at his island. He stood while his sister and Sangeeta sat on the stools. His first sip of morning chai was utterly life giving. They sipped their chai for a moment.

"What if I can help you secure your job?" Reena turned to face Sangeeta.

Sangeeta furrowed her brow. "Well, that would be fabulous. But according to my boss, no one will want me planning their wedding. She woke up to emails asking for other planners. And today is Sunday. She has suggested putting me on birthday parties, corporate events. As if—"

"You've heard of Asha Gupta?" Reena cut her off.

Sangeeta sipped her chai, nodding. "Influencer. Like up-and-coming?"

Reena nodded. "She wants out of her wedding contract at the fancy chain hotel she's been working with in town. But if she does that, her planner has threatened to quit."

Sangeeta's eyes bugged out. "Who would quit in the middle like that?"

"Well, this would be the second planner Asha has lost. She's very—particular."

"As one should be when planning their wedding." Her gaze drifted from Reena to Sonny and then out the small window.

"Right." Reena paused, giving Sangeeta a moment. "So, I've contacted her, suggested Lulu's as a backup if she leaves. Told her all about what we can offer her. She's thrilled and excited, but the one thing I do not have is a planner willing to take this project with only two months left until the big week."

"And you're here because…?"

"She asked for you."

"She what?" Sangeeta nearly dropped her mug.

Reena cleared her throat. "Well, it seems that the video-watching public thinks that you left your groom for—" she nodded at her brother "—true love."

Sangeeta widened her eyes and shifted the disbelief in her gaze from brother to sister.

"And," Reena continued, "she thinks it's adorable. Not to mention that your video has gone viral, and she would like to capitalize on the fact that *her* planner is the woman who chose true love over everything else."

"But that's not true. I didn't run because I was in love with Sonny or anyone else."

Sonny pretended the pang he felt at her immediate denial of feelings did not happen.

"It doesn't matter. All you have to do is let her believe that you did, and then pick up where the other planner left off. She can be quite the bridezilla, but it doesn't seem like you have many options. I'm sure your boss would be impressed that you were able to land Asha Gupta's wedding."

Sangeeta sipped her chai as she considered. The dazed look about her was gone, and she seemed a bit more like her normal self. "Lilliana would be thrilled. I'd have certain job security." She nodded as if convincing herself.

"See, it's a win-win. Here's the USB." Reena pulled out the drive from her wallet. "I set up a meeting for tonight in Sonny's restaurant." She glanced at Sangeeta's foot. "In case you couldn't walk far."

"You brought the file with you?" Sonny blurted out.

Reena grinned. "I knew she'd agree."

Chapter Eight

Reena's thumb drive was full of information. This bride had everything planned down to the smallest detail, and it did not seem like she had much tolerance for anything being off. Or for not getting exactly what she wanted.

Fueled with chai and whatever delicious food Sonny brought up, Sangeeta studied the documents until she knew them like the back of her hand. Excitement coursed through her. This was going to save her job. Tina brought her some professional clothing along with the information that Param had taken off. Presumably on their honeymoon. Tina had tried to stave off her parents, but they were not having it. Sangeeta finally texted them that she would meet with them later that night. She'd get an Uber after the meeting with Asha.

"But your mother is *not* happy." Tina had shaken her

head. "My mom is trying to keep her from losing it, but the truth is no one in the family really understands what's going on here."

"You're the best for doing this for me. I know it's a lot."

"Listen." Tina had clasped her hands to get her attention. "I want you to be happy. Just figure this out." Tina had squeezed her in a tight hug and gone back to the office.

Sangeeta considered herself warned. She would absolutely talk to her parents tonight, after she got this job. It would be easier if she could at least say she still had an income.

She intended on paying her parents back some of the money they had spent on this wedding. If she got the Gupta wedding, her cut would make a dent in that. The fact that Param was gone for now gave her a small reprieve in that she did not have to explain that video to him as well. She knew it looked bad. The way Sonny had looked at her for that split second seemed to imply there was something more than there really was. The reality was that though it looked bad, it really wasn't. She had not left Param for Sonny.

She showered and changed into her traditional black pantsuit with white button-down shirt, to be fresh for the meeting. Sangeeta was far from starstruck by influencers, but this one could help her, so she wanted to make a good impression. Reena had instructed Sonny to make a variety of his specialties for the meeting, to keep Asha in a good mood.

Sangeeta was seated in a corner of the restaurant with her computer open when Asha walked in. She was trailed by what one could only call a posse—a young woman who looked like her, must be her sister, as well as two exceedingly handsome men. She presumed one of them was the groom.

"Oh my!" Asha exclaimed as she entered the restaurant, looking all around, her beautiful face shining with pure delight. "How positively quaint." Sangeeta followed her gaze. With all that had happened, she hadn't really taken in the restaurant itself. Sonny had decorated the place so it had the feel of a street truck in India. He even had an old replica of a truck in the entrance. Asha smiled beautifully from ear to ear. "I love the casual, unpretentious vibe in here, don't you, Nila?" She squeezed the young woman's shoulders.

"I love it, Didi." Nila nodded enthusiastically. "We'll get some pics to post." Nila was simply dressed in a sundress and flat chappal. She little-to-no-makeup, her hair up in a messy bun, and so had that fresh-faced look of youth about her. As Nila and Asha chattered, Sangeeta found herself touched by the closeness the two women shared.

Asha was dressed in white jeans and a flowered long flowing angled one-shouldered top. She wore large earrings and bangles, and full natural makeup. She was stunning and she had good taste. Hence influencer.

"If the food is as amazing as the place, we're in for a treat." Asha nodded at Reena. "Thank you, Reena, for arranging all this." She gave Reena a welcome hug.

"My pleasure, Asha." Reena motioned to Sangeeta. "Asha, this is Sangeeta. Sangeeta Parikh, meet Asha Gupta."

Sangeeta extended her hand. "So nice to meet you,

Asha. Thanks for meeting with me. I'm sorry to hear that The Posh isn't accommodating your needs. I promise you that I will be able to see you through to whatever you want for your big day at Lulu's Boutique Hotel. I've been looking over your file, and you're quite thorough."

"I should be thanking you, for offering to take this on so last-minute." Asha quirked a smile at her. "I'm so happy to meet you. You are so brave, to run from your own wedding for true love." Asha placed her hands over her heart and shook her head. "So romantic. So completely Bollywood. Don't you think, Rahul?"

"Of course." One of the men stepped forward. Rahul was tall and broad and ridiculously handsome. "Very romantic." He put his hand on Asha's shoulder and leaned down to kiss her cheek. Asha flushed.

"Asha. I need to get back," Rahul said softly.

The light in Asha's eyes from Rahul's kiss dimmed a moment, before she turned her head to him and flashed a brilliant smile. "Of course. I'll see you tonight."

"Absolutely." Rahul kissed her cheek again, then nodded at Sangeeta. "Nice to meet you."

"You too," Sangeeta said.

Asha watched as her fiancé walked out, then turned back to Sangeeta. "He is always soo busy." There was a hint of sadness mixed in with the pride in her voice. "This is my brother, Akash Gupta." She grinned. "Akash is here for the food." She rolled her eyes in amusement, but again, Sangeeta could easily see the love she had for her brother.

Sangeeta shook his hand. "Nice to meet you. Have you met Reena Pandya?"

Akash turned his gaze to Reena. His smile grew

larger and his eyes lit up. "I have not had the pleasure." He extended his hand to Reena. "Nice to meet you."

Reena's eyes hardened as she firmly and quickly shook Akash's hand, her mouth pressed into a line.

Sangeeta and Asha sat down in front of Sangeeta's open laptop and got down to it. "You've got excellent decorators who are not bound to The Posh, so that should not be a problem. I assume your outfits have already been purchased?"

Asha nodded.

"And they are being adjusted as we speak?"

Asha shook her head. "Custom made."

Sangeeta flushed. Rookie mistake. "Of course. Let's review what we have. One week at the hotel for all your guests as they show up. Monday, Tuesday Wednesday for arrivals. Thursday night for your mehndi night. Friday morning is your grah shanti, Friday evening for the sangeet/garba and Saturday morning for your wedding and the evening for your reception and then, of course, the after-party. Sunday is the farewell brunch. Did I miss anything?"

Asha quirked perfectly colored lips. "You are quite efficient. No, you did not miss anything."

Reena brought out a tray of steaming mugs of chai for everyone. Kamila followed with a large platter of samplings from the kitchen. The aroma of chai was always comforting to Sangeeta, especially now, when everything had gone so…off-plan.

She sipped her chai, the milk and cardamom hitting her mouth like a comfortable T-shirt from her childhood. It buoyed her. Reminded her that she could be in control again. "The one thing you will lose when you leave The Posh is the food. I highly recommend Ginger and Cardamom to cater the wedding lunch and reception, along with their food truck, For Goodness' Cakes. I'm also pretty sure Divya Shah could do the after-party from that food truck. She specializes in both savory as well as sweet crepes, made to order. The other dinners are at restaurants, so none of that has to be changed. I will, of course, inform them of the point-of-contact change, once this is all official."

"Well, actually. No. I've changed my mind." Asha sampled a kati roll. "Reena convinced me it would be best if I kept all functions in-house, so it would be easier for my guests, and me—" she grinned "—since I could make the entrance I wanted by simply coming down the glass elevator. One of the perks of a smaller, boutique venue."

Sangeeta was already typing in her computer and nodding. "We will need food for those days, then. We can cater from local restaurants. And then we simply need to add to the decorators. They need to do the days leading up to the wedding at Lulu's as well. Shouldn't be a problem." She brought up the decorator's website, then turned her computer toward Asha. Sangeeta listened to Asha explain what she was looking for, as she filled one of the crunchy small puris with the potato and lentil mixture and sweet chutney, before dunking it into her bowl of spiced water, and then popping it into her mouth. The explosion of flavor was incredible. Pani puri was one of her favorite snacks, though she hardly ever went to the trouble of preparing it. And Sonny had outdone himself.

"How is it?" Asha asked.

Sangeeta nodded and widened her eyes while giving a thumbs-up as she chewed. Asha immediately made herself a puri and popped it in her mouth. Her eyes widened and she let out what sounded like a groan as she chewed. They both took a minute to enjoy the flavors.

Asha blurted, "Who made this food?"

Reena smiled. "My brother Sonny. It's his place."

"It's incredible. The pani puri, the kati rolls, the flavors—just the right amount of spice. I feel like I'm eating street food in India," she gushed. "I must meet him."

Reena coolly shrugged and stood. "Of course. I'll get him."

Sangeeta eyed Reena. She had only known her a day, yet Sangeeta had the feeling that something was up. Something only Reena really knew about.

Asha continued to ooh and aah over the food, and Sangeeta was unable to get her to focus on the computer. Reena returned shortly with a more than slightly irritated Sonny trailing behind her. He appeared to be muttering something only Reena could hear, but Sangeeta could absolutely guess what it was from the look on his face.

"Asha," Reena said, "my brother Sonny Pandya."

Asha looked at Sonny, her eyes slightly narrowed. She looked from Sonny to Sangeeta and back. "Wait. It's you." She waved a finger between them. She turned to Sangeeta. "He's the one you ran away for." She glanced at Reena. "You kept that quiet. Your brother is the guy."

Sangeeta opened her mouth to protest, but Reena got there first. "Well, they don't really want to go on about it, but yes. It's true."

Asha squealed. "How completely adorable. It's like

real-life Bollywood." She grabbed Reena's forearm.
"Oh my god! Can you imagine if I had them *both*? If
Sangeeta was my planner, and Sonny did my food?"

"I thought you were going with Ginger and Cardamom," interrupted Sangeeta. She didn't like the turn
this was taking.

"Well, yes, for the wedding day, but for the mehndi
and the garba, this would be fantastic! We could set
up booths—you'll come up with something. Anyway,
I must have them both. It'll all be in-house. I love it!"
She clasped her hands over her heart. "How positively
romantic to have two people so in love working on my
wedding."

"Oh no. I can't cook for your wedding," Sonny spoke
up.

"What?" Asha's face darkened as quickly as it had
lightened. She was clearly used to getting her way.
Sonny was unfazed.

"I can't cook for your wedding. Not to mention, Sangeeta and I are—"

"So touched you came today," Reena swooped in. She
passed Asha and went to her brother. She grabbed his
bicep and Sangeeta's hand. "Sonny, we forgot the patties, and Sangeeta Bhabi, can you come grab the lassi?"

Sangeeta Bhabi? Now she was Reena's sister-in-law?
Her stomach went into knots.

Sangeeta stood and nodded at Asha. "Be right back."
What the hell just happened?

Reena nearly dragged them through the kitchen and
to Sonny's office. She shut the office door and turned
to face them, with a smile. "We all need this." She nodded at them with the certainty of a businesswoman who

knew what she wanted. "Sangeeta. All you have to do is finish what was started and pretend to be in love with Sonny for a couple months."

"What?"

"And, Sonny," Reena continued as if Sangeeta had not spoken, "same. Pretend you two are a couple until Asha's wedding is over. And make food for the garba and mehndi nights."

She nodded at them both. "Okay. Great." She made to leave.

"Hold it," they both spoke in unison.

"What?"

"I am not cooking. And you know it," Sonny said to his sister as if Sangeeta wasn't even there.

Funny how that was where he put his foot down.

"I'm not pretending to be in a relationship with him." It was one thing to allow Asha to believe the comments in that video, but to actively pretend? No.

Reena inhaled deeply as if they were the ones being difficult. "Asha is enthralled by what she deems is your 'romance'—not to mention that video went viral, and that means more views for her if you both work with her." She turned to Sangeeta. "Just pretend for a couple months. Then you can quietly 'break up'—no one will notice."

Sangeeta did not speak as she mulled this over. The truth was, all she had right now was her job, and if she wanted to keep her job—this was her chance.

"You're not actually considering this?" Sonny turned to her.

"It's not my first choice, but if I want to have a job, I need Asha's wedding."

Sonny turned to his sister. "You set me up."

Reena pressed her lips together.

"I cannot believe you thought that would work. I am not cooking for that hotel."

"If you don't, there will no longer be a hotel." Reena sighed.

Chapter Nine

"This is your baby sister," his father had whispered as he had pointed to a tiny brown baby sporting a pink cap, lying spread-eagle in her crib, on the other side of the glass. There were a couple of tubes hooked to her and she just looked so fragile, Sonny couldn't imagine her fighting anything. He was four years old, and this was the first baby he'd ever seen.

"She is your responsibility to take care of, as her older brother," his father had said. "She was born a bit early, and that makes her a fighter. It is your responsibility to see to it that she is happy." His father had looked him in the eye. "Protect her, Sunil."

Young Sonny had nodded as his father's words embedded themselves into his very being. Little Reena needed him. He was overcome with love and affection for that tiny little person. She looked so alone and vul-

nerable in that crib with the tubes coming out of her. He vowed in that moment to always be there for her and not let any harm come to her. Over the years, as his parents worked odd hours to eke out a living, Sonny never strayed from his vow. Reena came to depend on him, and Sonny always put her first. It was the same when Jai was born. The age gap was larger, but Sonny automatically took over the care and keeping of his baby brother.

"So dramatic, Reena. I didn't fall for that when we were kids, and I'm not falling for that now." Sonny shook his head at her, making eye contact with Sangeeta.

"I'm not being dramatic." His sister's usual stiff professionalism fell away, and the light left her eyes. "Papa has not been able to make the loan payments to the bank for a few months. Business just isn't what it needs to be. They gave a grace period, but it's coming to an end. If we get this wedding, her followers will want to do events at our hotel. We'll get money from Asha. But the real money will come from the references. It's marketing, publicity. And people do things blindly when influencers recommend. We'll get people in, not just for big events, but for business, weekend getaways, the whole thing. This wedding could save us." She paused, and Sonny saw the true fear in her eyes as she continued. "If we can't pay this month, Papa is going to sell the hotel in order to keep the bank from taking over."

"It'll take time to find a buyer—" Sonny started, but his sister was shaking her head.

"He already has someone lined up."

"Who?"

"He won't say. Just that it's a good deal. The buyer

will own the hotel but wants nothing to do with managing. So, we would still be managing everything." Reena folded her arms across her chest. This was not acceptable to her. It wasn't acceptable to him either, but he lost his vote when he walked out.

"This is the reason that the chef quit," Reena continued.

Sonny narrowed his eyes. "What do you mean?"

"I mean, the numbers are low, and we barely break even. Papa had to cut Kiren's salary. This company has offered Papa a ton of money to sell before the bank takes it. The conglomerate would take over the note and the hotel, but Papa would at least end up with a nice chunk of money. Kiren got a better offer and bailed."

"I always told you Kiren would only look out for himself," Sonny grumbled. "And what about you?" Sonny asked. For as long as he could remember, Reena had talked about nothing else but running the hotel. Even as a child, she never played house, she played hotel owner, and took great pride in fixing up her hotel as she saw fit. That spirit still lived in her.

She shrugged and shook her head. "What about me?"

"You're supposed to own that hotel. It's supposed to go to you."

"Which is why I need this to work. Asha's wedding could be all the difference—at the very least, we'd be able to pay the bank the months we'd missed, and also be able to show them that we would be booked moving forward. Papa was ready to sell, and I begged him for this chance, and it's all I'm going to get. I'll do anything to make it work. *Anything.*"

"So, you want me to cook for this wedding, which

takes place at Lulu's, and for Sangeeta and me to pretend to be a couple and help you with this wedding. To save the hotel," Sonny stated just so he understood completely. If he didn't love his sister so much, he'd have to hate her for doing this. He didn't even know what to make of this whole faking-a-relationship-with-Sangeeta thing. He was so worked up about having to cook for his father's hotel.

Sonny had washed dishes in the main hotel restaurant kitchen when he was in high school. He worked the line when he was in culinary school, learning every aspect of the kitchen. When he graduated, he applied for a job as a chef in the kitchen and happily started where anyone else would have—at the bottom. When the head chef left, Sonny applied and jumped a few people to get the position. He was determined to excel. The chef who had left cooked classic food, which was wonderful, but it was getting boring. Sonny began making changes the minute he started working. He still offered the classic meals, but he added Indian food and then Indian street food as well as comfort food to the menu.

"What is all this?" his father had demanded.

"It's going to be fantastic for business, Papa. Right now, people have to go Edison for Indian comfort food, but I can give it to them right here in Baltimore."

"No. It does not fit with the vibe of the hotel," his father had insisted. "We need to keep the food the people want. Not introduce them to foods and flavors they are not familiar with."

"The menu is getting stuffy. Indian food is different, new flavors. Trust me, customers will like it. I'm even

thinking to set up a makeshift stall in the corner, facing the street so we can do 'street food.'"

"Just go back to whatever we had before." His father had been adamant. "This is not the way we want to go."

"Papa—"

"No."

His father had walked out of the kitchen. Sonny continued to do his thing. One week later, Sonny came in to find his nemesis from culinary school in his job. Kiren had had it out for him day one of school. He had gone so far as to sabotage Sonny's kitchen, but Sonny never could find proof of it.

Sonny had stormed to his father's office and into the middle of one of his meetings. "Are you kidding me? You hired Kiren—knowing that he sabotaged me in school."

"Kiren is doing what I asked." His father had remained unnervingly cool. "You still have a job. Kiren is the head chef. You can work under him."

"You're making a mistake," Sonny had warned. His father had not responded so Sonny had left. "I quit."

That still stung, even though it was close to a year ago. He gained little satisfaction in the fact that Kiren had just quit, seeing that the ship was sinking. But he was a sucker for his siblings. He'd practically raised them.

"Fine. This one time. For you. Let's make it clear— I'm doing this," he glanced at Sangeeta, careful not to make full-on eye contact, "*all* of this," then back at his sister, "for you." He was going to pretend to date a woman he actually liked. This was not going to end well for him.

Reena threw her arms around him, seemingly forgetting all her professionalism. "You are the best big brother."

"Yeah, I know." *She had no idea.* His heart thudded in his chest every time he glanced at Sangeeta. *What had he just agreed to?*

"Come on. Let's give bridezilla what she wants." Reena smirked.

They stopped in the kitchen to get more food and joined Asha and company.

Sangeeta put down a tray of potato patties, complete with cilantro chutney and tamarind chutney. Sonny followed with a small jug of mango lassi. Sangeeta poured a bit for everyone. "Well, Ms. Gupta—"

"Call me Asha."

"Asha." Sangeeta raised her lassi and everyone else followed suit. "To you and your wedding." She caught his eye and surprised him by sidestepping closer to him. She awkwardly placed her hand in the crook of his arm.

Sonny stiffened at her touch, a defense mechanism for sure. Asha narrowed her eyes at them. Now was not the time for defense. Now was the time to lean into his feelings. Every lie was better when based in truth. The truth was that her touch sent sparks through his body.

He inhaled and dropped his gaze to Sangeeta. She was looking at him with questions in her beautiful brown eyes. He took Sangeeta's hand in his and did what came naturally. Her bronzed skin was smooth as silk against the callouses on his hands. He brought his lips to the back of her hand and kissed it. She gasped and he met her eyes. She smiled and relaxed in his grip, moving closer to him. For a split second, he imagined that she was giving in to real feelings as well . . .

He caught himself. Of course she wasn't. She had been ready to marry another man yesterday.

He noted Asha's smile of contentment from the corner of his eye, before locking his gaze with Sangeeta's.

She raised her glass to him and dipped her chin as she gave him a small smile, a conspiratorial spark lighting up her eyes.

They had a deal.

Chapter Ten

Sangeeta relaxed into his hand and his gaze. His lips sent a zing through her arm and then her body that was unexpected to say the least. They were in this together. He certainly did not owe her anything, but this would be a win-win for their businesses. She wasn't sure exactly what his deal was with not cooking for Lulu's, but she didn't care, as long as he did. If they made Asha happy for the next two months, they were golden.

"Aw, aren't you two the cutest," Asha gushed. She nodded at her sister, who took a picture of them on her phone. "That'll be on my page soon. My wedding team. Reena, I'll sign. I will meet you at the hotel first thing tomorrow morning."

Sangeeta barely had a chance to take in Reena's relieved look when she heard a familiar voice.

"Sangeeta Amol Parikh." Her mother. Using her middle name. Neepa Parikh was a tough businesswoman, working side by side with her husband. In her late fifties, she could easily pass for a decade younger, if not two. She ate well and exercised and wore a sari and a classic long braid down her back, like armor. She made an intimidating figure on a good day. Today was no exception.

Sangeeta's insides jumbled. "Ma." Her mother focused on her hand in Sonny's. "Dad." Her father stood behind her mother. Where he always was.

"Sangeeta?" An arched eyebrow from her mother asked more than Sangeeta was prepared to answer.

"Oh. Are these your parents?" Asha asked.

"Um. Yes. Ma, Dad. This is Asha Gupta. I'm going to be planning her wedding." Sangeeta barely knew what she had said, because her mother was here for answers as to why she had run yesterday. Sangeeta was not prepared.

"Sangeeta! Are you on something?" Her mother's voice had risen a few octaves.

"Ma. I was coming over for dinner in a bit." Sangeeta actually squeaked. In front of a client. Ugh.

"Sunil Harish Pandya." A male voice with the same level of authority spoke before her mother could answer.

Sangeeta's hand was still in Sonny's, so when he stiffened, his grip on her hand tightened. She did not pull away.

"Papa," Sonny addressed his father, who had entered just behind her mother. "Did we miss dinner?"

Sangeeta turned her attention to Sonny's father, who was an older version of his son. He was fit and stood just an inch shorter than Sonny. His full head of black hair was lightly sprinkled with white, and he wore a suit with a level of comfort that indicated he wore them frequently. The only thing that was different was the intimidating intensity of his nearly black eyes.

Both parents now stood next to each other, piercing their children with similar looks of forced patience. A wall of disbelief and discontent. Sonny squeezed her hand harder.

Both his father and her mother spoke at the same time. *Yelled* would be a more accurate word.

"You seem to have lost all sense of what is right and wrong, young lady," her mother continued.

"How could you possibly be in love with Neepa and Amol's daughter, when you haven't seen her for months? I know you liked her then, but once she turned you down, I assumed you had moved on," his father added. Sonny flushed.

"Papa—"

"If you had feelings for the Pandya boy, you might have said something to…to…anyone! Rather than just run from the wedding! At any point during the planning, you could have spoken up," her mother continued. "We had tried to set you both up at one point." She nodded at Sonny's father for confirmation.

"We did." Harish Parikh confirmed.

"Ma—"

The two of them went on in this manner for another minute or so, no one getting a word in edgewise. Sangeeta held on to Sonny's hand and thankfully, he did not seem like he was letting go either. They really were in this together.

Asha watched, sipping her lassi, seemingly enthralled. She finally stepped in, all elegance and poise. "So nice to meet you, Auntie. I must say that Sangeeta must get her strength from you."

Sangeeta's mother turned her glare to Asha. "I'm sorry?"

"I mean it's not every day that a woman runs from her wedding because she's in love with someone else."

Neepa Parikh was a master of her facial expression, and that talent did not fail her now. Only Sangeeta saw the complete surprise and horror that flashed in her eyes before she covered it. "I see."

"Well, yes. She ran from her wedding to be with her true love." Asha gestured to Sonny.

"And Uncle!" Asha gushed at Sonny's father. "I'm so excited to be having my wedding at your hotel." She extended her hand to him.

"Is that so?" He turned to Reena.

"Yes, Papa. Asha and I were just scheduling a time for her to come in and sign papers. Sangeeta here is going to take over as the planner."

Uncle's gaze flitted over Sangeeta and to her mother.

"Harish Bhai," her mother addressed him.

"Neepa Ben. Amol Bhai." Sonny's father addressed her parents with some surprise, but recognition, nonetheless.

"It seems that my daughter left her wedding yesterday and came running here," her mother spoke to Harish Uncle.

"They are in love," Asha gushed, seeming to not notice the tension in the room.

"The scandal in the family—" Her mother started.

"Sangeeta," her father spoke gently to Sangeeta. "What has happened?"

"Dad," Sangeeta managed to squeak out. Sonny ran his thumb over her fingers, and she relaxed. Her breathing slowed and she swallowed. "I don't know. I was standing out there, waiting for Toral to open the doors, and I couldn't breathe. I just could not go through with getting married. So I ran." She took a sharp intake of breath and looked at Sonny. "I'm sorry. I'm so sorry."

Her father drew his glance over their still-clinging hands and nodded. "Okay, beti."

Her mother turned on her husband. "Okay? *Okay?* You spoil her. That is why this is happening. This is *not* okay. What will people say? What are they already saying? Not to mention the cost."

"And that video," Sonny's father added.

"And that video," Neepa concluded.

"That video—" Sangeeta's voice cracked.

"Is what everyone will see or has already seen," Reena interjected, coming to stand near them both.

"Who are you?" Neepa Auntie asked.

Reena extended her hand. "Reena Pandya. His sister."

"Well, Reena, that video only adds to the scandal. What am I supposed to tell our family? Param's family? Sangeeta, of all the things that you have done…"

"Well," Reena intervened, "the reality is that Sonny and Sangeeta are…together now."

Sangeeta's parents looked stricken. "Sangeeta?" her father asked.

"Well. I did come here from the wedding." It was the truth. But now she was lying to her parents. Not exactly the first time, but this was a big one. This was not "I did not smoke last night." This was something else entirely. It was harder than she'd thought it would be. But she'd made a deal. With the devil perhaps. But a deal nonetheless that she needed. If she had no job, she'd be back to being dependent on her parents. She could not go back to that. They could all tell their parents the truth after Asha's wedding.

"Why didn't you say something earlier?"

"I... I...didn't realize my true feelings until the moment was upon me." Keeping as close to the truth as possible would help here. "Once I realized how I felt, I had to go." Her voice went quiet. "So I ran. Dad, I'm so sorry. I'll make it up to you. I'll pay you back, I promise."

"Does Param know about Sonny?" Her mother eyed her still with suspicion.

"Um. No."

"His mother said he's gone on the honeymoon." Her mother said it as if she were dropping a bomb.

Sangeeta nodded. "Yeah. I heard."

She narrowed her eyes at her daughter. "You really love him?" She nodded at Sonny.

"Yes," Sangeeta spit out.

"So Auntie, Sangeeta is now with the boy you had chosen for her," Reena interrupted.

Neepa opened her mouth and then closed it, contemplating this information. "That is true." She looked around the restaurant as if considering this. Her gaze landed on Sangeeta, a small frown on her face. "But it doesn't help me deal with the Sheths, does it?"

Sangeeta shook her head.

"But I did choose well for you, didn't I?"

Sangeeta simply stared at her mother.

Sonny cleared his throat. "Sweetheart," he said quietly, "she chose well, didn't she?" Sangeeta turned to look at him. He silently encouraged her to go along with this line of thinking.

She turned back to her mother. "Yes, Ma. You did." She moved closer to Sonny so the sides of their bodies were touching now. She leaned a bit into the solidness of his muscles, gaining strength or maybe simply being held up. Either way, she was grateful. She definitely pushed away the fact that she *liked* leaning into his body.

Her mother pursed her lips at her. "We will address all that later. But how often does a mother get to be truly...*right*?"

Sangeeta narrowed her eyes, her stomach in fits. "What do you mean?"

"I mean why wouldn't I be happy to learn that my daughter is in love with the man I picked for her?" A smile had replaced the frown from a few minutes ago. Sangeeta would take it.

Asha looked at Sangeeta. "What? Your mom set you up?"

"Actually, we both did." Sonny's father decided now was the time to speak.

"We had introduced them some nine or ten months ago," her mother continued. "Sangeeta had told me she wasn't interested."

"Yes, well. Sonny seemed interested, but then..." his father shook his hands and bobbed his head. "I don't know what happened."

Silence thickened in the air.

"Well, yes, they introduced us. We didn't want the parental pressure to influence our relationship. We wanted to figure it out, on our own. But then Sangeeta said she loved Param and was going through with her wedding. Until today." Sonny, who really had not said much up until now, had a whole story for them. Sangeeta smiled at him. Keep it as close to the truth as possible.

"Is that true?" her mother asked.

"Yes." She nodded with what she hoped was confidence.

"So, we were right?" Her mother smirked, nodding at Sonny's father.

Because that was the important thing right now. For once, Sangeeta was grateful of her mother's ability to make every situation about her. "Yes."

"Looks that way," Sonny spoke as he squeezed her hand again. Right now, Sonny's hand felt like the only solid thing she had to hold on to. This was what happened when you went off-plan. You found yourself clinging to the hand of a man you hardly know, who was now your fake boyfriend. For better or worse, they were in this together now.

Asha was grinning. "This just keeps getting better. I cannot tell you how thrilled I am that you both are going to be handling my wedding." She looked at Uncle. "Your son is an extremely talented chef. I'm very excited to have him cooking for the wedding."

Uncle pressed his lips together and looked his son over. "Full of surprises today."

Sonny said nothing, keeping his expression stoic.

"Well, I must be going," Asha said. Sangeeta had to

hold herself back from begging her to stay. "Reena, I'll see you in the morning. Nice to meet you, Uncles and Auntie." She turned to Sangeeta. "My brother, Akash, will set up a time for us to go over decor and such."

"Sangeeta." Her mother spoke as Asha left. "Gather your things and let us go."

Sangeeta stared at her mother. "Go where?"

"To your Masi's house, where else?" Her mother said as if it were obvious.

Oh, hell no.

"Ma. I can't come to Masi's house." She forced herself to sound logical, even. Not whiny. "I'm working. This wedding has just been given to me, I don't have time to go back and forth from Masi's house to here."

"Where will you stay?"

"Well, since Param has gone, I'll stay at the apartment until I find my own place." *That made sense, right?*

"Don't be ridiculous, beti—"

"I'm not, Ma." Sangeeta squared her shoulders and lifted her chin. She was not leaving. "I'm staying in town."

Her mother pursed her lips and looked around the room, skepticism oozing from her. "Uh huh. Amol." She said without looking at her husband. "Let us go."

Sangeeta's parents turned and left, somewhat appeased by her promises that she would keep in touch with them.

Now that she was not focused on Asha, she noticed that Akash was much more casually dressed than the fiancé had been. He was in jeans and a black T-shirt and was clean-shaven, while Rahul had sported that "just the right amount of scruff" look.

Akash approached Sangeeta with a small smile as he pulled out his phone. "Hi. Sorry, sometimes my sister forgets that we don't all work for her and her followers." He handed her his phone. "Just give me your number and I'll put us on a text chain with Asha and work out the time and location of the meeting. I'm sure Asha would love if Sonny could make it, as well."

"Um. Yeah. Sure." Sangeeta took his phone and entered her number.

"Perfect." Akash offered a genuinely kind smile and nodded at her. "We'll be in—" He stopped suddenly and glanced behind her. "Touch." His smile broadened to the point that Sangeeta noticed he had two dimples.

Sangeeta turned around. Reena had come up behind her. Akash extended his hand to her. "Nice to have met you," Akash said.

Reena cleared her throat. "Yes, you too." She dismissed him with a nod.

Odd. Reena should be bending over backward for Asha's brother.

Akash nodded at Sonny's father and left.

Sonny turned to face his father. "What brings you here, Papa?" He had seen his father at the required family dinner every other Sunday evening, but the man had never set foot in this restaurant.

"Well, Reena called to say you were both too busy to come to dinner tonight. But then, Jai showed me that video of you and Sangeeta." He nodded in her direction. "So I thought I'd come and see what was happening. Clearly, an exciting time for you."

His father did not believe them. Not for one hot second. Whatever, as long as he didn't say anything, what he knew or didn't was irrelevant. And he wouldn't. His father was smart enough to understand how Asha's wedding could help the hotel.

"Yes, Dad. And how fortunate that Asha Gupta wants them both for her wedding?" Reena went over and kissed his cheek. His father allowed it, and Sonny saw him melt just a bit. Reena wasn't even the favorite. It was Jai. But no one begrudged Jai that special spot.

"Hmm... Yes. Fortunate." He narrowed his eyes at his children. "Your mother will want to be discussing this with the both of you. She's finishing up at dinner. She'll be in touch," he said as he turned and left.

A pit formed in Sonny's stomach. He may have his issues with his dad, but his mother was the force he dealt with.

Sonny looked at his sister. Even Reena showed signs of minor panic. Fantastic. They were lying to everyone. The three of them just stared at each other for a moment, the weight of their deceptive undertaking lying heavy between them.

Sonny looked down and realized he was still holding Sangeeta's hand. Not that he minded.

"Oh. Sorry." Sangeeta had followed his gaze and then quickly freed his hand from hers.

"No problem." He muttered. He flexed his fingers. Empty now.

"Listen," Reena said, regaining her composure. "We really need to sell this—so the truth is on a need-to-know basis. You two have to look like a couple everywhere you go, because Asha has followers everywhere."

"Yeah. We got it, sis," Sonny grunted.

"I mean *everywhere*."

Sonny narrowed his eyes at her. "What are you getting at?"

"You have to live together." The words tumbled so quickly out of her mouth Sonny wasn't sure at first what she had said.

There was a beat of dead silence until they both started protesting.

"Are you kidding me?"

"My apartment barely holds me!"

Reena put her hands out like she was trying to calm wild animals. Which maybe she was. "Stop!"

She looked at Sangeeta. "You just told your parents you're not going to your masi's. You told Param you would move out. Where will you live?"

Sangeeta pressed her lips together and shrugged. She had no intention of going back to Param's apartment.

Reena turned to Sonny before he could say anything. "You're hardly even in your apartment. You're here most of the day, before you trudge upstairs and collapse without even eating." She shook her head at him. "A chef. Who misses meals." She rolled her eyes.

Sonny wanted to protest, but she had him. He shot a glance at Sangeeta and found her looking at him. Her jaw was set, and her mouth pursed. She wasn't any happier about this than he was.

"If you do this, Sonny, it's not just for me. The restaurant will get tons of publicity. Sangeeta, this will save your job, ten times over. It's two months. One huge event. We move forward with this and all three of us will get something out of it. As soon as Asha's wedding brunch is done, you two can go your separate ways. I promise." Reena laid it out.

Sonny glanced at Sangeeta. If they were in it, they were in it. He tried not to think about how soft her skin had been, or the thrill that had gone through him when he'd kissed her hand. This was fake. At the end of two months, Sangeeta would be out of his life. He just had to think of it as a business venture.

Sangeeta spoke first. "Fine. I'm all in. I'll pretend we're together if that's what it takes."

"Me too," Sonny said. He turned to Sangeeta. "Welcome home."

Chapter Eleven

Sangeeta typed away at her computer, sitting on a stool at Sonny's kitchen bar. Her AirPods were in as she chatted with another one of the vendors, confirming the location change as well as the increase in supplies needed. Sonny was currently cooking down in the restaurant and most likely would be all day. Sangeeta needed to get her thoughts organized before heading over to Lulu's Boutique Hotel later today to get a lay of the land, so to speak, before her meeting with Asha tomorrow. She hadn't yet done a wedding at Lulu's, but as a planner, she'd visited a few times to simply dream about how she would run a wedding there.

Lilliana was more than satisfied with Sangeeta being able to plan Asha Gupta's wedding, so she had job security for the time being. In fact, Lilliana was eager to get Sangeeta the help she needed. Sangeeta simply asked for Toral, who was her regular assistant. Her boss was more than happy to assign her Toral as well as provide continued access to the contacts Lilliana had made over the years.

The buzzer rang, indicating that someone was at the back door. Sangeeta limped her way down to open the door.

Tina barged her way in past Sangeeta and up the steps without speaking. Sangeeta inhaled. She'd seen this coming.

She limped back up the steps behind her cousin into Sonny's apartment and shut the door, just as Tina spun around and faced her, her poker straight dark hair falling like a sheet. "Tell me you seriously left Param at the mandap because you had feelings for Sonny."

Sangeeta paused for a beat. Tina wasn't technically need-to-know.

"Don't you even think about lying to me, girl." She narrowed dark eyes and shook her head. "You know I can see right through you." Her words were calm and to the point, but her eyes flashed an undeniable warning. They were sisters and this information was required.

"Of course not," Sangeeta answered. It was the truth. Her feelings for Sonny were not part of the consideration when she ran. Nothing was. Just the lure of freedom.

"Then what the heck is all this?" She held up her phone and scrolled. The video, the picture, Asha Gupta's Instagram and Snapchat feeds.

"I'm saving all that I have left. My job." She went on the offensive.

"Are you kidding me? You and Sonny are faking? Have you learned nothing?"

When Sangeeta gave her a quizzical look, Tina continued. "Anita and Nikhil? At my wedding? Secrets have a way of becoming public, sister. Then they blow up in your face."

"That was different," Sangeeta scoffed. "They were in love with each other, they just didn't know it."

"And you and Sonny?"

"Me and Sonny are not secretly in love with each other." Forget that when he kissed her hand yesterday, every cell in her body exploded.

Tina stared her down.

"Seriously, Teen. I have to move out of Param's apartment, so I have no place to live, and Lilliana was ready to fire 'the wedding planner who ran from her own wedding' because no one wanted me to plan for them. Until this. Asha thought I ran for true love. Now I have a job and place to live, at least for a couple months."

"You're living here?" Tina eyed the surroundings as if seeing them for the first time. "Cute."

"It makes sense." Sangeeta moved into the apartment as if she were already comfortable here. Nothing could be further from the truth. She was a creature of habit. She liked her bed. She liked her stuff.

Tina shook her head. "No, it doesn't. Nothing about this makes sense. Come live with me."

"I'm living here, for now. We have to make it look good."

Tina sighed and paced the small apartment for a moment. "Where did you sleep last night?"

"On the sofa." If you could call tossing and turning sleeping.

Tina pursed her lips. "He didn't offer you his bed?"

"Actually he did—"

"With him in it?" Tina smirked. "He's very hot."

Sangeeta gave her a withering look.

"Come on. Don't tell me you can't *see* him." She smirked at her. "Those glasses," she whispered, widening her eyes. "At least get *benefits*."

"I just left my wedding—two days ago. I'm not ready for *benefits* or anything else. He offered to take the sofa. I insisted that I take the sofa. It's his house. His bed." Besides, the notion of sleeping in his bed even alone gave her thoughts she knew she shouldn't be having. *Talk about benefits.*

"Uh-huh."

"Tina. I need this job. It's my only way out of the mess I have created. If it means faking that I'm in love, then that's what I am doing. Two months and I'll be out. I may even have some money to pay my parents back."

"Fine." Tina rolled her eyes.

"You cannot tell anyone." Sangeeta was firm.

"I got it." Tina sighed, plopping herself down on the sofa. "This is ridiculous. You know this is ridiculous."

"I'm trying not to think about it too much."

Tina let out a large sigh. "Fine. What do you want me to do?"

"Not tell anybody."

"Done. What else?"

"Drive me over to Param's so I can get some of my stuff."

"Sure." Tina paused. "You know he's on your honeymoon."

Tina nodded at her cousin. "How many times do you need to tell me?"

"With Rani." Tina raised both eyebrows, waiting for her reaction.

Sangeeta plopped down on the sofa next to Tina, letting that information sink in. She was surprisingly unaffected by the news that Param and Rani had gone to the islands together. "She's his best friend. At least it wasn't wasted."

Tina looked at her, one eyebrow raised. "Okay, then." Tina stood. "Let's go get you some clothes."

Sangeeta rode up the elevator, the familiar smell of lavender air freshener clawing at her stomach. She had no reason to be nervous going back to the apartment. Param wasn't even going to be there. In fact, he had told her to go get some of her stuff. But the dread settled into her, nonetheless. She had hurt a good man and the guilt was a stone in her heart. The elevator doors opened with a ping and a swoosh, and she walked down the familiar white-walled hallway on patterned gray carpet. The unit doors were a chic black, many with welcome mats out front.

She nearly walked past her doorway, as the wreath she had hung on the front was no longer there. The stark number 31 simply stared at her, naked and unwelcoming.

"Come on," Tina said. "Let's just do this."

Sangeeta nodded. She opened the door with her key and let them both in. She was immediately ensconced in the mixture of her perfume with his cologne. She had not stayed here in the last week leading up to the wedding. Her mother had insisted she be with the family at Seema Masi's.

"Let him at least be surprised a little bit to see you in the mandap," her mother had demanded.

Even though she had not been there, her perfume still lingered as if it were part of the air in that space. Funny because now that she was here, she wondered how she had ever belonged here at all. She flicked on the light. Everything was neat, not pristine. It was clear that someone still lived here. The pillows were fluffed on the sofa, but an empty highball glass sat on the coffee table, next to the remote control and an almost empty bottle of bourbon. Param's lesson plan book was next to it. She walked into their bedroom and found her suitcase at the foot of the bed where she'd left it packed and ready to go for her honeymoon. Param hadn't touched it. But then, why would he?

Sangeeta unzipped the hard-shell bag and looked at the sexy lingerie and bathing suits that were suitable for the island honeymoon they had planned. She zipped it up and pulled out its matching, larger bag from the closet. Into this, she put work clothes and shoes, sneakers—whatever she could fit. It would all have to be moved out at some point; she just didn't have time right now for all that.

She rummaged through her drawers and pulled out a few keepsakes, tucking them carefully into her bag.

Within half an hour, she was packed and ready to go. She was already a stranger in this apartment that felt like it belonged to a different lifetime. To someone else. Only her scent belonged here.

"Don't you want your perfume?" Tina asked, eyeing the expensive bottle on her side table. "You love this stuff."

Sangeeta shook her head. "I'll buy something new." She grabbed the bag she'd packed, and then at the last minute the "honeymoon" bag, and followed Tina to the elevator.

Chapter Twelve

Sonny dragged himself up to his apartment. It had been a slow day, with hardly a handful of customers. He knew there would be days like this, but it still frustrated him. He didn't want to admit it, but the run-in with his father yesterday had him on edge as well. It was going to be harder than he'd thought, cooking for the hotel.

It was close to midnight when he entered his apartment. He was about to flick on the lights when he saw Sangeeta's form asleep on the sofa in the wan light of the streetlight coming in the window. He just needed a quick drink of water before he collapsed on his bed. He was taking soft steps toward his kitchen, when his foot hit something hard and he went tumbling over it and onto the floor with a thud and a loud groan as his bottom hit the floor.

Someone screamed. There was the sound of scrambling and then the light was on. Sangeeta stood over him with a baseball bat in her hands and a crazed look in her eyes.

"Whoa. Whoa. It's me!" he shouted as he held up his hand and squinted in the sudden light.

"Sonny?"

"Who the hell else would it be?"

"Sorry." She lowered the bat. "I didn't know… Anyway, a woman has to protect herself."

"Where'd you get the bat?" Sonny growled, still on the ground, trying to regain some dignity. He was going to have a bruised foot and butt.

"My apartment."

He looked at what he had fallen over. "I suppose these suitcases came from there as well. Why are they in the middle of the hallway?"

"What hallway?" She spread her arms, still holding the bat.

"Whoa!" Sonny ducked his head, his eyes bugged out. "This hallway, from my room to the kitchen."

"That is not a hallway." She lowered the bat as if she just noticed that she had it.

"It's also not a storage facility," he said irritably.

"Well, maybe if you had worn your glasses—"

"I'm wearing contacts. Steam fogs the glasses," he groaned as he tried to shift his weight to his other butt cheek.

"You going to stand up?" Sangeeta still stood over him in a T-shirt and pajama pants, her hair completely disheveled. How she could manage to look that amazing and be so irritating at the same time was his first thought. His second thought was how he was going to stand up without looking like an idiot in front of her.

He moved to get his legs under him.

"You okay?"

"I'm fine." He stood, but he had definitely bruised his right butt cheek. He walked to kitchen for that water.

"You're limping."

"Well, I think I broke my ass tripping over your suitcase."

"Oh." Sangeeta's mouth was pressed together, and she was shaking, her eyes glowing with amusement. "I'm sorry." A giggle escaped her, and she clamped her hand over her mouth.

"Are you laughing?" he asked, biting the inside of his cheek as a reluctant smile made its way to the corners of his mouth. Sangeeta giggling was an adorable sight to behold. "At my pain?"

She shook her head. "Of course not." Another giggle escaped.

"Because that would be —" he fought the smile, but it was now becoming a laugh, because damn it, Sangeeta was contagious "—insensitive."

She nodded. "You are correct." She seemed to have swallowed all the laughter. "I wouldn't want to be a pain in the ass." At this point, she lost it at her own pun and laughed outright. There was nothing "adorable" about it. Sangeeta laughed with her whole body, raucous and unabashed. She was magnificent. "I'm sorry. But you were sprawled—and now you're limping, holding your—" She nodded at his butt and flushed. Though he wasn't sure if the flush was from laughing or looking at his ass.

Sonny couldn't help it. "You should have seen yourself. With the bat. And your hair." He was exhausted and he should be annoyed, but he started laughing too. "No one... No one is going to mess with you."

Then they were both doubled over in laughter, and they fell to the floor, gripping their stomachs and desperately trying to sip air. They finally caught their breath.

"I am—" she cleared her throat, and brought her knees to her chest "—truly sorry about this. We'll work out a system. I'll get a night-light or something."

"Or—" Sonny caught her eye still sitting across from her, in his "hallway" "—you could take the bed, and then I can turn on the lights when I get home. And not be threatened by your baseball bat."

"No." Her answer was too quick and sure.

"What? I'll wash the sheets. It makes the most sense. I never roll in earlier than midnight. It's easier if I sleep out here and you sleep in my—in the bed."

"I don't want to put you out," she said.

"I think we're past that, thanks to Reena. Besides, I agreed to this as much as you did. I can't walk in the dark for two months." He shrugged. "Think of it as—I don't know. Don't think about it too much." He laughed. He offered his hand to her. She took it and they pulled each other up. "Come on." He limped into the bedroom and grabbed clean sheets. Sangeeta limped in after him. "Well, aren't we quite the pair?" He ripped off the old sheets and started to put new ones on.

"We aren't really a pair," she said as she secured the fitted sheet around the corners on her side. She wasn't giggling anymore.

Sonny secured the corners on his side, then floated

the top sheet to Sangeeta. "That's true." He watched her across the bed as she tucked in the sheets. She was right. Yet here they were, putting sheets on his bed. Where she would be sleeping.

Sangeeta looked everywhere but at him while she tucked in the sheets. As if she were thinking the same thing.

There was no way she would be thinking how amazing it would be for him to crawl over to her and pull her into these clean sheets with him. And see how dirty they could make them. The thought flitted across his consciousness before he could stop it.

"Well. I'll just…let you get back to sleep, then." Suddenly as awkward as a twelve-year-old on his first encounter with a girl and convinced she could read his thoughts, Sonny attempted to leave the room without getting near her. Somehow, his room shrunk to half its size. It became near impossible for him to avoid being close to her.

"Yeah. Sure." She backed away from him as he moved to the door. "I…uh…have an early day. I should—" she motioned to the bed, but then flushed   this time not laughing "—sleep. I should sleep." She didn't look at him.

"Yes. Sleep." He scurried out of the room.

It was going to be a long two months.

Chapter Thirteen

Akash never actually texted her. It was Nila, Asha's younger sister, who sent her a text and set up a time to meet at Lulu's Boutique Hotel. Sangeeta inhaled as she walked through the door that the bellhop had opened for her. It was a beautiful morning with a summer sun, and a spring breeze. Days like this were rare and only found in May in Maryland. She was working on a huge wedding that would secure her career. What could possibly go wrong?

Reena greeted her as soon as she entered. "Hey. How's it going, Sangeeta Bhabi?" She said it like that was Sangeeta's real title.

"Your brother and I are not really together. You don't have to call me that when Asha's not here."

"I don't want to slip up. As far as I'm concerned,

you and my brother *are* really together for the next two months," Reena said. "Come on, let me show you Lulu."

Reena took Sangeeta around the hotel, showing her the two large ballrooms where the functions would be held. Sangeeta made notes on her iPad, jotting down ideas for efficiency as they came to her. She would need to set up a walkthrough with the decorators, and have Amar and Divya come take a look as well. Amar was the head chef and owner of Ginger and Cardamom, as well as Anita's brother. Divya ran For Goodness' Cakes, a dessert food truck, and she made amazing crepes. The two were engaged and worked together, and they were an adorable couple. They had also been the caterers for her wedding. Sangeeta was trying to get them more business, but she was dreading the awkward moment when she saw them again.

Sangeeta shared some of her ideas with Reena and was met with enthusiasm as well as thought-out methods of improvement.

"I love these ideas, Sangeeta." Reena beamed. "My brother seriously lucked out when you ended up at his door."

"Lulu's Boutique is incredible. I know you say your parents own it, but your influence is everywhere." Sangeeta glanced around. "I love the little touches of Indian decor you have added."

"Thanks." Reena sighed. "I always felt like the decor was rather sterile, it needed some color. Big changes are overwhelming for my parents, so I add a statue here, a splash of color there." She grinned. "Sonny and I have similar visions. We want to incorporate our culture here. Mom and Dad are more about fitting in with all the other boutiques. Not appearing 'ethnic.'" She shrugged. "I'm not talking about throwing saris all over the place, but Indian food, decor that celebrates who we are, I'd love to see that here. Our Ba taught Sonny how to cook, but she taught me how to put on a sari. Her home was always beautifully decorated. I just want to incorporate some of that here." She fixed Sangeeta in her gaze. "My parents are coming around, but it's a slow process. They so needed to fit in when they first got here, it's almost like they're afraid to be too different."

Sangeeta clasped Reena's hands in hers. "It'll be worth it. This wedding will just be the beginning." She was starting to really enjoy Reena's company. They had a lot in common. "So… Asha's brother, huh?"

"What about him?" Reena was checking a detail on her iPad and didn't even look up.

"Um, hello. The way he looked at you." Sangeeta smiled at her new friend.

Reena waved a hand. "He can look at me however he wants. I do not have time for all that."

"Hey, ladies!" Asha's singsong voice came from behind them. She was accompanied by Nila. "Time for what?"

"Anything but work," Reena quipped with a smile. "Good to see you." She hugged Asha.

"You need a life, dear," Asha reprimanded.

Reena waved her off. "My work is my life."

"You sound like Sangeeta." Toral chuckled as she joined them from behind Asha. "She always said work was her life. And now look at her." Sangeeta's assistant nodded at her and she flushed.

Asha rolled her eyes with a smile. "I've got an hour,"

she said as she hugged Sangeeta. She posed with both of them, and Nila took a picture. "What do you have for me, Sangeeta? Oh, but wait—how is your guy?"

"Oh. He's great." Sangeeta nodded enthusiastically. Ugh, she was horrible at this. How was she supposed to act like she was in love, when she never really had been. It had been much easier to pretend when Sonny was there with her.

"Well, hello," a familiar voice called from behind her as a warm hand rested at the small of her back.

"Sonny." She turned to him, a smile coming to her face unbidden. "What are you doing here?"

"Nila asked me join you so we could coordinate," he said softly, close enough that she felt his breath on her ear, looking into her eyes as if he was thrilled to see her, as if this was the most normal interaction.

There was nothing normal—or real—about this interaction. But that didn't keep her from getting goose bumps where his lips nearly touched her ear or from melting where his hand touched her back.

"Perfect." She met his eyes. He side-smiled at her, holding her gaze. She cleared her throat. "Good thinking, Nila! It's always easier when the chef is here to coordinate."

"Amar and Divya will be joining us as well," Sonny said.

"I was just thinking I needed them to come see Lulu's." Sangeeta grinned at him.

No sooner did she utter these words than the pair strolled up, hand in hand. Amar stood tall next to Divya, murmuring something only she could hear. Today he was wearing a Ms. Marvel T-shirt under his open chef's whites. Divya had her hand in his, and bumped his shoulder with hers at whatever he said. Her hair, once cut in a trendy pixie style, was now long enough to push back with a headband, though she still sported the blond tips.

Sangeeta flushed as she realized this was the first she was seeing them since she'd ditched the wedding five days ago.

"Hey, guys," Amar said as they walked up.

"Hey." Heat rose up Sangeeta's face as she addressed them. "I am…so…so very sorry for…everything. You all worked so hard and then I—"

"No worries." Divya shook her head. "Didn't anyone tell you?"

"Tell me what?"

"The Sheth family stayed and partied anyway. Your grandfather paid and insisted they enjoy the food." Divya brightened. "We got a whole lot of business from that night, and the extra food we donated." She shrugged. "Granted, it wasn't ideal, but it worked for us."

Sangeeta gaped. Param had not said anything. Or even Tina. Sonny pressed his hand against her back. She looked at Toral, who shrugged. "It hadn't come up."

"Oh, great, then," Sangeeta managed.

"Though it looks like you have moved on." Divya smiled at Sonny.

"Um. Yeah." Sangeeta nodded and turned to look at Sonny. "Something like that." Sonny's hand remained at her lower back, and right now he pressed gently, as if to support her. The effect was wonderful. She stood straighter, smiled wider, all as she leaned ever so slightly into his hand.

"Something like that, indeed" said Amar, glancing at his friend.

"Let's talk food," Sangeeta said. "Asha only has one hour."

Chapter Fourteen

Sonny was tempering spices for a dish when someone called to him from the door to his kitchen. He could barely hear over the clanging of pots, the constant buzz of the exhaust fan and the sizzling of spices. Not to mention the chatter of the cooks working the line.

"Sunil Pandya!"

He whipped around because the voice sounded just like his mother. He relaxed when he saw it was sister. "What's up?"

"When are you done?" Reena called loudly as she got closer.

"Never." He turned back to his spices.

"Seriously."

"I am serious." He turned back to the stove.

She sighed. "When do you close today?"

"One hour."

"Perfect. Meet me out front at ten thirty. Make sure you shower and put on something nice."

He frowned at his sister as he kept rolling out tepla. "No."

"Yes. You're going on a date."

He moved the round disc to the hot pan and started rolling out another one. "With who?" Though a spark of excitement shot through him because he knew exactly who.

"Who else?"

"Sangeeta?" He laughed as he flipped over the flatbread on the stove and sprinkled oil around its edges, getting a satisfying sizzle. "She'll never agree."

"She already did."

Sonny turned to face his sister. "She agreed to go on a date with me?" He really should not be so excited by this prospect.

"Just meet me outside at ten thirty." Reena left.

Sonny was showered and dressed by ten twenty. His sister had said dress nice, so he had put on dark jeans and a navy button-down, untucked. He usually wore jeans and a T-shirt with his whites, so this was dressed up.

It wasn't that he was trying to impress anyone.

He loitered in his apartment for an extra ten minutes so as not to appear too excited about the prospect of a date with Sangeeta, fake though it may be. Where was Sangeeta anyway? He left his apartment at ten thirty and was out front by 10:33.

"You're late."

He heard her matter-of-fact lilt before he saw her.

Of course Miss Plan would be on time, and then fault him for tardiness.

"I was..." He stopped as he got closer to her. She was a flawless beauty in a sleeveless shimmery dress with a high neckline. It just grazed her figure, coming up a few inches over her knee. The dress was incredibly sexy considering that it revealed very little of her. She had on spiky heels that looked dreadfully uncomfortable, especially since he could see the bandage on the side of her foot. But he couldn't deny the effect the heels had on her strong, curvy legs. Sonny instantly found himself wondering how he would get the dress off her. "Busy."

"We're all busy, but we manage to show up on time," she snapped. And then he remembered that he did not care how she looked.

"How are you not in pain?" he nodded at her feet.

"I'll manage." She quipped.

He sighed and looked around. "Where's Reena?"

"You want your sister to come on a date with us?"

"At least I would have someone to talk to."

"Ha." She smirked at him.

They stood there looking at each other.

"Well?" he said.

"Well what?"

"Where are we going?"

"How am I supposed to know? Reena said you were taking me on a date because Asha was concerned that we did not have enough social media presence."

"She said I...?" He pointed to himself. Damn his sister. "She just told me to shower and meet here."

Sangeeta sighed deeply and mumbled to herself as

she pulled out her phone. "I'll see if I can get reservations somewhere."

Sonny's phone buzzed. Text from Reena. An entire itinerary for the night. "Uh—hold that. Reena has planned for us. Looks like drinks and dinner followed by dancing."

"With you?" Sangeeta seemed panicked.

"So it would seem." He glanced at her shoes, by way of her amazing legs. "Hope you brought flats."

Sangeeta lifted her chin and threw back her shoulders. "I told you, I'll manage."

Just then a car pulled up and rolled down the window. "Uber for Sonny Pandya."

Sonny grinned at Sangeeta and opened the back door. "Come on. Reena's paying."

Sangeeta sighed heavily but got in the car. Sonny slid in next to her. She smelled amazing, like flowers and something he could not quite name.

The Uber driver seemed to know where they were going, so they sat quietly for a moment.

"We should maybe take a selfie?" Sangeeta suggested. "Isn't that what couples do?"

"Yeah. Sure." Sonny pulled out his phone and held it at arm's length, capturing them both in the frame. They smiled, and he took the picture. He held out the phone again and turned as if to kiss her cheek and tapped the phone. He was careful to not actually touch her cheek with his lips. Simply kissing her hand had sent zings through him. He wasn't going to go through that again.

He showed it to her, and she shrugged, turning away from him in the dark. A few minutes later they pulled up to Maximón in the Four Seasons hotel. Sonny got out and held the door for her as she exited. He took her hand and they walked into the hotel to the restaurant. Their fingers intertwined, fit perfectly, and she did not try to let go of his hand.

"This place is beautiful," whispered Sangeeta, leaning into him. "I've only been here as a planner, for bridal showers and such, but the food is amazing."

Sonny simply nodded as he watched her take in the live music and the Saturday night vibe. She had curled her hair and it now fell in luxurious waves down her back, framing her face. She gently shook her hips and shoulders to the beat, almost involuntarily. The dress swayed with her. He couldn't tear his eyes away, even when she turned to him and gave her first genuine smile of the evening. He returned the smile, squeezing her hand. This date might not be so bad after all. Though it was a good thing Reena was paying. He most likely could not afford this place.

"Ooh! There you two are!" Asha Gupta, decked out in a hot pink form-fitting off-the-shoulder dress, was waving to them from a table just outside the main dining room.

"What?" Sangeeta whispered.

"No idea," he whispered back. They looked at each other, smiles as fake as their relationship plastered to their faces.

"Don't you two look adorable!" Asha gushed as they approached. "Nila. Take a snap of us."

Before they knew it, they were seated with Asha's group, which consisted of her sister, Nila, and Nila's date, a gorgeous young woman named Payal, Rahul, Akash and another woman, Snehal, who appeared to be Akash's date. The wine flowed and the food was almost as continuous as the picture taking.

A couple of glasses in, Sonny leaned over and draped his arm around Sangeeta's chair. As if she were really his. She side-eyed him, but nestled closer into him. This was all fake. For show, for Asha. He had to remind himself that he didn't even really like Sangeeta. A little voice inside his head said that if he had to remind himself of that, maybe it wasn't true.

Nah. It was true. It had to be.

Sangeeta had bolted away from him last summer without a kernel of remorse. And now she ran from another man. She was trouble. End of story.

He withdrew his arm and put some space between him and Sangeeta. The surprise on her face was fleeting, and quickly replaced with indifference. See? He was right.

"Oh! Salsa dancing!" Asha squealed as she looked out on the street. Sure enough, couples were salsa dancing to live music, just on the other side of the hedges that separated the outdoor tables from the street. She grabbed her fiancé's hand and stood. "We have to!" A reluctant Rahul stood to indulge his fiancée.

"Well, we're not going out there alone." He nodded at the table. "You're coming too."

"Of course!" Asha beamed. "Come on!" Nila and Payal stood and followed Asha and Rahul.

Asha led Rahul around the low hedges and onto the street. Sonny glanced at Sangeeta, who had started standing up. "Don't worry," she said. "I know how to salsa. I'll show you."

Sonny smirked at her and stood. "Uh-huh. Okay."

He nodded at Akash and Snehal as they too stood to join the crowd. Once on the dance floor, he and Sangeeta faced each other.

"Okay. You put your hands here and here." She placed one of his hands on her hip and took the other lightly in her hand. "Now step closer to me." Sonny obliged. She smelled of spice and flowers. "Okay, now," she whispered, "make it look like I'm teaching you. Because I have no idea what I'm doing beyond this."

Sonny grinned at her. "You want to fake dance in our fake relationship?"

"That's right," she hissed. "We need this."

"Well, I can only fake one thing at a time." With that, he clamped one hand onto her curvy hip, gripped her hand with his other, and pulled her to him so their bodies touched. She gasped as he stepped forward with his right foot, tapping her left foot to move backward. She followed as he led her through the salsa, a look of complete disbelief on her face. Almost as if she couldn't believe her own body was moving, as much as she couldn't believe that it was him who was moving it.

Sangeeta was not a quick study of dancing, but Sonny found he didn't mind, as that meant he could keep her body glued to his for the duration of the dance. The music was over before he was ready, and when he stopped, Sangeeta also seemed surprised that they had stopped moving. She was flushed and flustered and avoided his glances. They stood shoulder to shoulder, and he whispered, "Make it look like you like me. Asha's taking pictures."

She turned to him, a huge smile on her face. She

wrapped an arm around his waist and leaned into him. "Thanks for the dance lesson."

He was frozen to her. He did not want to move from this most perfect of places. Lights flashed, then Sangeeta pulled away, smiling. "There you go," she muttered.

"You two are the cutest!" Asha floated over to them, Rahul trailing behind. "Nila, Payal, come. I'll take a selfie and get all of us." She tucked her sister and Payal to her side as Akash and Snehal joined their selfie. Asha tapped with precision. "Perfect."

The music started again, and with a squeal, Asha dragged Rahul back to dancing. Sangeeta grabbed Sonny's hand. "Don't stop now. I was just starting to get it."

Chapter Fifteen

Sangeeta had two left feet. She could move to a beat, but if there were steps, she got flustered and tripped. Except for tonight. Sonny was quite patiently teaching her to salsa, and not only was she getting it, but she really liked it. It was probably the wine, she told herself because not only was she dancing, she was enjoying Sonny. But that couldn't be right. She had broken up with Param literally a week ago. And she had been ready to marry him. No, it was the wine and the faking. Besides, she could enjoy a guy's company and it didn't have to mean anything.

They were friends. That's all.

But they weren't. They irritated each other. They were forced together by a common goal and that was all. She stiffened in his arms, determined to keep her distance.

"Asha is watching," he whispered, that hint of a smile on his face, the one that said he was conspiring with her and he liked it. The smile that intimated a bond between them. His hand, warm and strong on her hip, guided her. "Like this." He raised his voice, loud enough to be heard, but his eyes danced with their secret, and her heart raced in response.

She followed his lead, which basically meant moving her body so that contact with his hand remained constant. Easy enough. *Hot enough.* "I'm dancing." She laughed, surprised with herself. "I'm doing the salsa."

Sonny grinned at her. "Don't think about it too much."

"Why? This is fabulous—ah!" She missed a step and nearly fell. Luckily, Sonny still had his hand on her hip and caught her before she reinjured her almost healed foot.

"That's why. Don't think about the steps." He took her hand, returned his to her hip and began moving again. "Just feel the music and move." She followed and stopped thinking. She felt the beat of the music and moved her body to it. She looked at Sonny as he looked at her, and everything else fell away.

The music ended and the surroundings rushed back to her in a wave of laughter and clanging dishes. Sonny stepped away from her and the moment was gone.

"Oh my god!" a young woman near them squealed. She looked from her phone to Sangeeta and back. "It's her! It's the Runaway Bride." People turned to stare. Heat rushed through her body.

"It's you, right?" The woman came up to her, her phone turned toward Sangeeta for confirmation that the woman in the red choli running from her wedding was indeed her.

"Well, um…" She glanced around. It was hard to breathe. Sweat beaded on her upper lip. Asha was encouraging her with a nod of her head. Sangeeta copied the nod. "Yes."

"I knew it! I knew it!" the woman squealed. She held up her phone for everyone to see. "It's her!" She turned back to Sangeeta. "Can I have your autograph?"

"What?" Was this woman serious? Sangeeta's heart pounded in her chest. It really was too warm here. "Um…well." She looked around but saw no one she knew. She took a step toward what she thought was the exit, but there were so many people around. All with their phones up, all shouting things at her.

Suddenly, Sonny was at her side, his arm wrapped protectively around her. "Hey. Follow my lead," he whispered low and close to her ear.

She nodded.

"Oh! That's the guy she ran away for." The woman honestly needed to let it go. "Isn't that right?"

Sonny ignored the woman and pulled Sangeeta tighter to him. "Come on." He guided her away from the crowd and away from the restaurant. They moved quickly, ignoring the disappointed groans from the crowd that had formed. Once in front of the restaurant, Sonny led her into the crowded street and away from the hotel.

A few blocks away, he released her, but they immediately fell into step.

"Close escape," she managed as her breath returned and her heart rate began to return to normal.

"Asha may not be happy, though." He was looking straight ahead of him as if he hadn't just held her close. Or maybe he regretted holding her like that.

"Oh. It seemed like everyone had a phone up. There must be a few pics of you 'saving' me." Sangeeta made the air quotes. "She'll be fine."

"I didn't save you."

"I know. It was a photo op." She inhaled deeply.

"Well." He shrugged. "I saved you a little."

She raised an eyebrow at him. She did not like having to be saved by him, or anyone else.

"You were panicking. I've never seen you like that." His voice was quiet, serious.

She continued walking. He walked beside her in comfortable silence.

"I'm an introvert. I hate crowds," she spoke quietly. As an introvert, this was not something she revealed readily, but there it was. "Sometimes I panic."

His turn to raise the eyebrow. "Really? A wedding planner who hates crowds. And runs from her own wedding. Ever consider that you might be in the wrong field?"

She gave him a withering look, though she was unable to completely repress the smile. "I like the planning part, the organizing, the putting-everything-in-its-place sort of thing. The execution," she sighed, "I could do without."

"So have someone else do that," Sonny suggested.

"It's like you don't even know me." She smirked at him. "What if they mess it up?"

"Ah!" He nodded. "I forgot you like the control part too."

She pursed her lips at him. "Not as much as you do."

"What? Not true. I'm super laid-back." He walked beside her, at her pace, as if there was nowhere else he'd rather be.

She stopped short. "I call BS. You are a control freak in the kitchen."

"What?" His eyes opened wide in complete disbelief. "I have two sous chefs."

"Ha." Sangeeta chortled. "I've heard you, Bossy Pants telling the cooks how to boil water."

"I did no such thing." He shook his head. The evening was warm and while the streets were far from quiet, it wasn't the bustle of Harbor East.

"Dharm." Sangeeta deepened her voice. "Put the water in the pot and put the heat on medium high. It will boil."

"I was going over the specifics of the chai recipe." He bit his bottom lip trying to hide his smile, and Sangeeta flushed with how handsome he was, even in complete denial.

"You were going over the basics of boiling water—to a chef."

He stared at her, brown eyes amused. "So maybe we both have an issue with control."

A taxi approached. Sangeeta raised her hand and it stopped. "Come on. These shoes suck."

Sonny got into the cab behind her and gave the cabbie an address.

"That's not home."

He melted a bit right there as she referred to his place as "home." Like a key fitting into a lock, it clicked perfection. It felt right.

"Sonny?"

He grinned at her. "I know. I want to show you something."

Sonny sat back in the cab and watched Sangeeta. Her hair was down, and some of the curls had come out, lying longer over her shoulders. The shimmery dress rode up just enough to reveal some toned upper thigh that glistened a dark brown silk in the passing streetlights. It was all he could do to not run his fingers along that skin.

"Where are we going?" she pressed him.

"We'll be there in like five minutes." He snapped his gaze from her body to the window. "You'll see."

The cab drove around the Inner Harbor area. The sky was a dark navy, with pinpoints of light. The water glistened in the neon lights and people were everywhere. The hour was late, so mostly the party and after-party crowd made their way around now.

Sonny reveled in the intimate space he was now sharing with Sangeeta as she looked out the window, clearly trying to divine their final destination.

The cab slowed down.

"We're going to the Science Center?" She looked at him, puzzled.

"How about just enjoying the surprise instead of trying to figure it out?"

"Where's the fun in that?" The cab stopped in front of the Science Center, and Sonny got out. He held out his hand as she exited the cab, and to his surprise, she took it.

She looked up at the sky, then at him, comprehension on her face. "Oh."

Sonny and Sangeeta had walked along the beach talking almost nonstop, long after the sun had set. The navy sky was clear, the moon piercing it with a waning sliver of crescent, allowing the stars to have the sky.

Sonny had been aware of every step, every breath that Sangeeta took. He was acutely aware of the cool air that grazed his hand as her hand would swing past. What he had been most focused on was the heat from her hand when it stopped near his. It shouldn't have really been a thing, him reaching out to take her hand, but she had been up front with the fact that her fiancé had just broken up with her, and Sonny knew even then that he did not want to be the rebound guy. If he had been paying closer attention to where he was walking, he wouldn't have stepped on the dried starfish.

"Ow." He hopped on one foot, and scooped up a couple of the small dried starfish.

"You okay?"

"Fine. Just these." He opened his palm and her eyes widened. "Stars in the sky and on the beach. Take them."

She took one and left one for him.

He laid out the towel he had brought. "Here."

They had lain down on the towel, next to each other, the space between them filled with the electricity of their not touching.

"If you look right at that bottom corner of the moon—" he raised his hand to point, and she had followed his gaze "—and go over a bit. There. See?"

He had looked to see if she was following and had found her staring at him. She swiveled her head quickly as if she hadn't been looking at him and turned her attention to the sky. "Yes."

"That dot is Mars. And the other dot is Jupiter."

"So cool." She sounded in awe. After a pause, she turned to him with a smirk on her face. "I mean, it's cool but they seriously look like dots. Probably be better with a telescope."

He had nodded his head and said nothing, just stared at the sky.

She wrinkled her nose, still lying on the towel next to him, the scent of her sunscreen mixed with the salty air of the ocean imprinting themselves on his brain.

"They're so small and far away." She whispered, reverence in her voice. "Kind of makes you feel a part of something huge, but we're just so small too."

"Exactly."

Her eyes lit up her crooked smile. "Is there seriously a telescope here? At this hour? Don't you need an appointment?"

He nodded. "Yes. And I took my brother's appointment." He'd owe Jai hugely, but her hand was still in his. He tugged on it. "Come on."

They took the elevator up to the observatory where the telescope was. There, they gazed at the sky through high curved windows, while they waited their turn to get a chance to use it.

"Do you come here a lot?" Sangeeta asked, her eyes concentrating on the heavens.

"Not as much as I would like to. The restaurant keeps me busy."

"You bring dates here?"

"I have never brought anyone here," Sonny said.

"So you *do* date?"

Sonny focused his attention on her and was debating a response when their names were called out. It was their turn. He gladly explained how to use the telescope, allowing Sangeeta to view first. Her gasp nearly took his breath away.

"That's incredible." Her eyes widened and she allowed her natural smile through, a genuine awe about her.

"I know, right?" Sonny moved the scope a bit and was rewarded with another gasp of delight, followed by a barrage of questions.

He took his turn viewing and answered what he could. They took turns for the duration of their allotted time, and too soon, it was someone else's turn.

Sangeeta was animated and bubbly and full of questions, most of which he could not even answer.

"I'm an amateur at this." He laughed.

"Not to me. This was amazing." She bumped his shoulder. "Thank you."

As they went down the elevator, Sonny arranged for the Uber to pick them up. She glanced at him and flushed. "I saw your starfish on your desk."

He lifted his gaze to her eyes. Deep brown and huge, they were her tell. She wanted him to say why he had kept that small souvenir from their time together. Did she still have hers?

The elevator dinged as they reached the ground floor and the moment was gone. Sangeeta limped a bit as they exited the elevator.

"You okay?"

She shook her head. "No problem. I borrowed these shoes from your sister. While they are adorable, my cut makes it hard to walk in them."

"You borrowed them from my sister?"

"I borrowed the whole outfit from her."

"Oh. Right." He had almost forgotten that they were on a fake date. Or they had been. "Well, the Uber is just outside." He nodded at the door. "I'll carry you."

"You most certainly will not. I can walk." She took a few a steps and cringed.

"I think you are at the end of your time in those shoes, sexy though they are." Oops. Did he say that out loud?

"I'm fine." She took another step and cringed.

"You're going to reinjure that cut. Luckily it was small and on the side, but you don't want that reopening."

"Well, I'm not letting you carry me."

"Well, you do remember what happened the last time you went barefoot?"

"I also know what happened the last time you carried me. I ended up in a fake relationship with you." She folded her arms across her chest.

"Seriously? That's your concern?"

She shrugged and nodded.

"Not a problem." He approached her and squatted down in front of her. "We'll do it piggyback."

"This dress is short."

"No one will see. Come on, the Uber will be here in three minutes." He tapped his shoulders. "Hop on."

She groaned but did as he said. She wrapped her arms around his neck and her legs around his waist. Sonny stood, taking hold of her legs under each knee. Her skin was as soft as promised. Maybe he should not have offered this. Too late. Her body was pressed to his and he tried not to think about which parts of her were against which parts of him.

He turned his head to the side and found his face next to hers. Not helping. "All set?"

"Mmm-hmm."

He carried her halfway down the block to where the car was meeting them. She clung to him as if afraid he would drop her.

He chuckled. "I'm not going to drop you."

"You never know," she said as she squirmed higher onto him. "I'm not exactly one of those tiny petite girls."

"Whatever that means."

His unease had nothing at all to do with whether she was petite or not, and everything to do with the fact that the front of her body was completely smashed up to the back of his. Luckily, the Uber was there when they got there. He put her down because he could not very well hold her all night, but as soon as she was on the ground, he missed her body against his. He quickly opened the door and motioned for her to sit.

"I can carry you up to the apartment," he said as she limped into the car.

"It's okay. You can just run up and get my sneakers," she quipped as she scooted over.

He nodded. Probably best for everybody involved.

Chapter Sixteen

There was no way she was getting on his back again. She steeled her expression into one of impassive indifference, when her mood was anything but. All she wanted was to climb him again, but those were hormones talking, she told herself. Though she was also impressed by the fact that Sonny had not so much as broken a sweat or taken a heavy breath while he carried her. He was stronger and fitter than she had given him credit for.

She had left Param dangling exactly one week ago. This was supposed to be a fake relationship, for their mutual professional benefit. And so it would stay, if she had anything to do with it. Besides, how could she possibly have any real feelings for him, so soon after her breakup?

No. Anything she was feeling right now was

hormone-induced lust. Sonny was very, very attractive. Anyone would have lustful feelings toward him. Giving in to that jeopardized their whole plan. Any chance she had to repair her life started with her having a job. Right now, making Asha Gupta happy was her best bet. It was the only reason she'd agreed to this date and allowed Reena to make her up. The fact that she enjoyed the way Sonny had looked at her when he first saw her was, well, not just beside the point, but something she had to forget altogether. This was not only unplanned, she'd already hurt him once.

She waited at the front door of the restaurant while Sonny ran up to the apartment.

"Sneakers." He announced as he unlocked the front door from inside. Without a word, he knelt down and put them on her. She gripped his shoulder for balance, pointedly ignoring the way his muscles moved beneath her hand as he slipped on and tied her sneakers for her. He had long since rolled up the sleeves on his button-down.

"Oh. So much better." She nearly groaned as she walked toward the stairs to the apartment.

"You're limping."

"It was a long night in those shoes," she said. "Dancing and whatnot."

"If you can call it that." He chuckled.

"What?"

"Your dancing…it lacks…rhythm."

"Are you kidding me?" She riled up. He was, of course, correct, but she wasn't about to admit it.

"Um no." He grinned as he opened the door, allowing her to enter first.

She limped past him and straight for the bathroom. "For that, you'll have to wait until I'm done with the bathroom."

Sonny tossed and turned all night on his sofa, thoughts of Sangeeta in that dress, and out of that dress, keeping sleep from him. And as it always happened, just as he was finally finding sleep, his phone started buzzing nonstop.

He picked up the phone and saw a text from Reena. Immediately, he put it down, determined to ignore it.

Didn't she ever sleep? It was 3:00 a.m.

His phone buzzed again. If he didn't respond to texts, she'd call. He picked up his phone and read the message.

You two ditched Asha! She's highly irritated! You cannot do that.

He typed fast: We did not ditch her. People were all over us.

He watched as the three dots floated, waiting for the response he knew was coming. That's the whole point!

You did not tell us we would be out with them.

Details.

It was me. Sangeeta was replying. He hadn't even noticed she was on the chain. I might have had a small freakout. Sonny got me out of there. I'll make it up to her.

Reena's reply was swift and to the point. See that you do.

Damn but his sister was bossy. Sonny opened a separate text window and texted only Sangeeta: You still awake?

Nothing. Not even the three dots in a bubble. Disappointment washed over him and he was about to give up getting an answer when the three dots appeared. His heart raced, and he shifted to a sitting position. She was typing.

Sangeeta: Can't sleep.

Sonny: Me neither.

Had he responded too quickly? But the dots appeared almost immediately.

Sangeeta: All that dancing LOL. And the stars. I really loved the stars.

'The stars are incredible.' He typed. "But not as great as seeing them from the beach.' He erased the last line. He was revealing too much. "I'm glad you enjoyed our 'date'. He added the laughing emoji. Keep it light.

This time the dots appeared, then disappeared. Sonny found himself staring at his phone like a lovelorn teenager, nearly holding his breath. Then the dots appeared, and he was embarrassingly giddy.

Sangeeta: I did have a good time. You're a good dancer.

The dots appeared again. You never told me why you kept that starfish.

Sonny waited a moment before answering. We had good times on that beach. Do you still have yours?

The dots appeared for a few a seconds, then disappeared.

Sangeeta: Good night.

Sonny: Good night.

Chapter Seventeen

Sangeeta ended up not really having to do anything about Asha. By 8:00 a.m., there was a picture of Sonny holding her close and escorting her out of Maximón all over the internet. A little creepy, but it did the job. Asha texted that all was well, and that she totally got how someone new to all the attention could get freaked out. Sangeeta promptly put the night where it belonged in the back of her head. She had work to do. She didn't have time to ponder her feelings about last night, or her text exchange with Sonny.

Sonny was already down in the kitchen cooking. Sunday mornings were busy for him. Sangeeta worked better at Lulu's, where everything was, so she could visualize things more easily. Or so she told herself. The reality was that she was too distracted by Sonny to stay in the apartment.

So as soon as she was showered, she grabbed her files and computer and called an Uber. She stopped in the kitchen while she waited for her ride.

"Hey." Sonny glanced at her over his shoulder from the stove.

"Hey." She tried to sound light and airy, but as soon as she saw him all she could think about was his hand on her hip and her legs around his waist.

"Busy day?" he nodded at her various bags and smiled, as he wiped his hands on his apron.

She relaxed into his easy tone. "Super busy. Even on a Sunday." She chuckled and shook her head.

He reached for the chai pot on the stove, and poured some into a to-go mug. "This will keep you going."

She took the mug and inhaled the spicy freshness of it as she twisted the lid shut. "Thank you." She caught his eye and for a moment, the kitchen fell away and it was just them.

"Your, uh... Uber is probably here." He nodded at her phone, and the moment was gone.

She nodded and left.

Reena had found her space to work, nothing more than a small cubicle, but it was hers. The chai was a magic elixir as far as Sangeeta was concerned. She spent a very efficient day making phone calls and setting things up. Before she knew it, it was 6:00 p.m. Her stomach growled and she realized that she had barely eaten. Reena walked in just then with a cardboard takeout box.

"Oh. You are the absolute best. I'm starving. Your timing is perfect." Sangeeta closed her computer and stood, doing a few stretches before she sat down to eat. The aroma hit her, and her stomach complained, so she cut her stretches short. "Oh my god. Is this pav bhaji?"

"From my brother." Reena had a smug knowing look in her eye that Sangeeta chose to ignore.

"Oh. That's—nice. But no one is looking."

"His exact words were, 'She's probably working away and didn't eat. She's got to eat.' He had Dharm deliver it to the hotel."

Though she hardly wanted to, Sangeeta melted a bit. He had thought about her and what she might need.

"Well, then I guess I better eat." She took out her phone. "But first, let's get some mileage out of it." She took a picture of the food and posted with the caption, "When your boyfriend feeds you amazing food!" She started to delete "boyfriend," but she knew Asha would want it there. She tagged the restaurant as well as the hotel and her company and Asha.

Reena nodded her approval as she headed out.

"Aren't you going to join me? There's plenty." Sangeeta motioned to the extra chair in the small space.

"I suppose I could spare ten minutes for my fake bhabi."

"Perfect." Sangeeta beamed. They ate out of the containers, each bite a sensation of spice and sweet, bitter and sharp, all in a perfect blend.

"So you're the one who runs this place?" Sangeeta sacrificed a bite to say a few words.

"Not officially, but it's all I have ever wanted. I'll do anything to save this place." Reena squirted fresh lemon over the spiced vegetable and potato mash.

"Obviously."

"I know it seems like I'm a hard-ass, but I see the potential here. I can grow this place. My parents had wanted it to feel like luxury, like a treat away from home. But I think people want that luxurious feeling along with the feeling of home. It's a tight balance, I know, but I can make it happen."

"That's how Sonny wants to feed people. Good food, comfort."

Reena fixed her hazel eyes on Sangeeta and smiled at her. "You get it."

"You're very close, you and your brother."

Reena nodded as she swallowed. "He took care of us while our parents built all this."

"Did he?" Sangeeta perked up at getting more information about Sonny, a new angle she hadn't yet seen. She gave in to her excitement for a moment.

"Yes. He was always there for us. After school, dinner, etc. Even drove us around to our activities and such. He's the best." Her fondness was clear.

Sangeeta nodded as she listened to Reena tell stories about "big brother Sonny" and how he took care of her. This part of Sonny was sweet and loving and fierce. He obviously would do anything for his siblings.

"He's four years older than I am. My dad loves to tell me the story of our first Rakshabandan. I was still a baby, six months old. I 'tied' rakhi on his wrist and he gave me this plush bear." Reena's eyes moistened as she looked into the past. "I took that bear with me, *everywhere*. Whenever it was washed, I would stand by the laundry room until it came back to me." She laughed.

"You still have that bear, don't you?" Sangeeta teased.

"Busted." Reena laughed. "But that bear was always

part of my life, just like Sonny. As I got older, I learned he had given it to me, and I loved that ragged little thing even more. It was like having my big brother with me even when he wasn't there."

"I still have my first Rakshabandan present, too." Sangeeta confessed. "Tiny little gold stud earrings."

"Adorable."

Sangeeta took her last piece of bread and used it to scoop up whatever remaining bhaji she could, before popping that last bite into her mouth. "Your brother can *cook*."

Sangeeta was satisfied, grounded. She looked at the empty carton. Comfort food indeed. Her phone buzzed, interrupting her moment of zen.

Param. Her heart raced and she felt the blood drain from her face.

"What? Is everything okay?" Reena sounded concerned.

"I don't know. Param is back in town and he wants to meet."

Reena's eyes widened as she stood. She lifted her chin at Sangeeta. "Don't hurt my brother."

Sangeeta furrowed her brow. "Not possible. We're faking."

Reena set her mouth and left.

Sangeeta gathered up her things, her mind racing. The peace she had felt from Sonny's meal and listening to Reena's stories about him was all but gone. She slipped her computer and her files into her cross-body suitcase, grabbed her to-go cup and left her little "office." She crossed the lobby for the main doors and was stopped in her tracks by her parents and grandfather.

Dada smiled warmly and her panic dissipated some. "Hi, Dada. Ma. Dad."

"We need to talk." Her mother didn't ever beat around anything.

"Sure." Sangeeta looked around. There was a small sofa set open near the fireplace. It seemed to be away from the main lobby. "Let's sit there." She led the way. All three of them? This was not going to be a fun conversation. Though she wasn't sure what was left to discuss. She had offered to pay them back as much as she could for the wedding. Dada had seen to it that the vendors were happy and would simply keep their credit until there was another function. Read: Sangeeta's wedding.

"Beti," her mother started once they were seated. "What is going on?"

"I'm working."

"You know what your mother is asking, beti," her father said softly.

She did. She swallowed. "I'm happy with Sonny."

"You have moved in with him?"

"Of course." She said it like it made perfect sense that a person should run from their wedding and move in with another man immediately.

"Sangeeta. Do you really love him, or is this some sort of rebound, clinging thing?"

Sangeeta sat straighter in her chair. "I do not rebound, or cling. This is what I want right now." She'd pull out the rebound thing after she and Sonny "broke up." Her mother would enjoy being right, again.

She glanced at Dada, who did not seem to have much to say. "Dada?"

He smiled. "Beti."

"Don't you have anything to say?"

"Bring him to dinner." Dada's voice held all the comfort of her childhood.

"What?"

Dada stood. "We are all staying at Seema Masi's. Pick a day and bring him to dinner. If you care about him enough to leave your wedding and move in with him, we would like to meet him. Officially." Dada nodded at his daughter and son-in-law and they stood.

Sangeeta plastered a smile on her face. "I'll text you a date." She felt her grandfather's gaze on her as they departed.

She plopped down on the sofa. This was getting complicated.

And now she had to meet Param.

Sangeeta dragged her feet down the hallway of her old apartment building. Familiar scents of lavender—gag—and jasmine—heaven—swept by her as she passed the doors of her neighbors, whom she barely knew. She stood in front of unit 31 staring at the bare door as if it belonged to someone else. It had been nine days since she ran from this life, and yet she barely recognized it anymore.

She knocked on the door even though she had the key in her bag. Sounds of shuffling reached her from inside before Param opened the door.

The Param of her old life was also missing. The man who greeted her had unkempt hair and a slight tan, wearing a T-shirt and shorts. On the plus side, he appeared less frazzled than he had the day of their unmet nuptials. At least the deer-in-headlights look seemed to be gone.

"Sangeeta." Her name on his lips held the weight of pain and anger. No less than what she deserved. Though she could not remember how her name had sounded on his lips before. What she did know was exactly how her name sounded when Sonny said it, in its many iterations, irritated, angry, puzzled and mocking. Param stepped aside and she walked in, a guest where she had once lived. The apartment was basically as she had seen it last, minus the empty alcohol bottles.

She was still scanning the area when Param held his phone up to her. "What's this?" He wasted no time. He scrolled through photos of her with Sonny. Him helping her escape Maximón in his arms. Dancing salsa, their bodies touching. Tagging him as her boyfriend an hour ago.

Crap. Of course he'd have seen all this upon his return. "Um… I can explain." But could she? Could she trust Param with the truth? That she was faking to save her job, which she might lose since she ran away from marrying him?

"Can you? Because it looks like you've got a boyfriend one week after you didn't marry me." Param's voice was rough and harsh and everything she deserved.

She opened her mouth, but he interrupted her.

"Were you seeing him?"

"What?"

"Were you seeing him—" Param's voice shook with anger "—while we were together?"

Her heart sank. "No." She took a few steps toward

him. He backed away from her as if she could physically hurt him. "Why would you… I would never…"

"That's what I had thought. That you would never cheat. But how else do you explain all of this? How else do you explain this level of intimacy this fast?" Param shook his head. "We were supposed to be married. You ran, and the next thing I know is that you're seeing this guy. What else am I supposed to think?" He shook his head. "Don't even try to deny it. These pictures are proof enough."

He stopped and looked at his phone again, swiping through the photos. "I didn't look at my phone the whole time I was gone."

"I thought Rani went with you."

"She did." He glared at her, daring her to say something about it. "As soon as I landed, I turned on my phone, and there you were. Everywhere. You and him. At first, I thought it was a mistake, coincidence. After all, he's a chef, you're a wedding planner. It seems you are both working on Asha Gupta's wedding."

"Yes," she jumped in. "We are." Her voice sounded lame even to her.

He paused, then turned his phone to her. It was a photo of them looking at each other while salsa dancing. She hadn't even known that the picture had been taken. "But then I saw this."

She and Sonny are facing each other. One of their hands is clasped in the other's. His other hand is on her hip, her other hand is on his shoulder, with barely an inch between them. She'd had no idea that they had been so intimately close while dancing. She had been trying to follow his steps. But their physical proximity wasn't even the damning evidence.

Her chin was tilted up to him, her eyes fixed on his. His head is tilted slightly down, he's looking into her eyes. They both have small smiles on their faces. She remembered that moment. Sonny had been telling her to let go of the steps and just feel the music.

"Just look at me. Let the music move you."

She had done as he asked, and with just the slightest pressure on her hip, he had guided her through the dance. Whoever snapped that shot caught an intimate moment between two people. If it hadn't been her, Sangeeta would have sworn she was looking at someone else.

The woman in the picture is looking at the man like she's in love with him.

She opened her mouth to deny it, but nothing came out.

"How long were you with him? No, I don't even want to know that. What I want to know is why you didn't even have the decency to come to me before and just break up with me, instead of running to him from our wedding." Param's anger was calm, as he always was. Param did not lose his temper. It was one of the things Sangeeta loved about him. Had loved.

His anger didn't blow up, it seethed. That's what was happening right now. His beautiful dark eyes were hardened coal. His lips set in a line. His jaw ticked. She had done this to him. She had hurt him like this, and her heart ached for him. She wanted to put it right, but she had no idea how to do that.

"Param, I—ran because…because… I could not

marry you." She inhaled. "It had nothing to do with—we're faking," she blurted out.

"What?"

"We're faking." She exhaled and continued, spilling her words into the air. "Sonny and I are faking. We're not really together. That influencer thought I ran from you to Sonny and she thought it was romantic and so she wanted me to plan her wedding and no one else did, and I was going to lose my job, so Sonny and I agreed to pretend to be together so Asha would let me plan her wedding and I could pay my parents back."

"But you're living with him."

"To make it look good."

Param stared at her for a long moment. "That's ridiculous. The Sangeeta I know would not do that."

"I'm not the Sangeeta you know. Any more than you are the Param I knew. I ran from our wedding because I wasn't ready. Because a big part of me knew you weren't the one. I wish I had realized it at any time before that moment, but I didn't, and for that, I am truly sorry. You and I don't belong together like that." She looked at him. "You know it."

He softened.

"We weren't right for each other. We deserve to be with people who we belong with. I love you. But I don't want to be married to you."

He ran his hand through his hair and paced a bit more, clenching his jaw, every so often stopping to stare at her. "So you and this chef are not really together?"

She shook her head.

"And it's supposed to be a secret, that you are faking?"

She nodded.

He threw his hands up. "Whatever." He glanced at his phone, then looked at her, sadness in his eyes. "Are you sure you're faking? Because I'll say this, you never looked at me the way you're looking at him in this picture."

Chapter Eighteen

Sangeeta had quite easily gotten into the habit of going down to the kitchen for her morning chai before heading out to the hotel. It seemed silly to make it upstairs when the aroma of cardamom, cinnamon and clove reached her, tempting her to just grab a cup.

Her conversation with Param from the day before still weighing on her mind, she gathered what she needed for the day and made her way down to the kitchen, where she knew Sonny would be, already a few hours into his day.

She'd be lying if she didn't confess to herself that watching Sonny work was an exercise in peace. The grace and confidence of his movements was fluid. She had to watch closely to see where one thing ended and something else began. He gathered ingredients here, tossed them in there, gave a stir as the delicious aromas filled the air around her. He flipped the naan, stirred a pot and gave an order to Dharm. All seemingly without effort. Sonny didn't cook. Sonny was part of the kitchen. As vital and important as the stove, pots and pans and the spices. Without him, the kitchen was just a place to make food. With him, it was an area of creation. Little though she wanted to admit, seeing Sonny in his element each morning was fast becoming one of her favorite parts of the day.

Sonny had come to expect her each morning as well. So when she walked in today, she was surprised to find that her chai wasn't waiting for her as it usually was. Sonny was alone, and decidedly not calm.

"Hey. What's going on? Where's Dharm?"

"Oh, hey." Sonny turned away from the cutting board, where mounds of onion and vegetables waited to be chopped. He pushed up his glasses. "Oh, sorry, I forgot your chai." He moved toward the pot on the stove.

"That's okay, I can get it." She went to the stove and poured herself a mug. "You're wearing glasses." He was very handsome in glasses. In fact, she preferred them on him. Not that she should have a preference. They were faking.

"I'm out of lenses. And Dharm is out sick." He shook his head. "And I couldn't find anyone to come in."

She sipped that life-giving elixir that Sonny did so well. Anita swore that Nikhil made the best chai, but Sangeeta would beg to differ. "I'm not the best cook, but I can chop like nobody's business."

Sonny shook his head. "Nah. Don't you have your day planned? Meetings with Asha and my sister. My dad?"

She nodded. She did. She had a huge day planned. But looking around the kitchen, and peeking out at the crowd, she didn't know how Sonny would manage all day, single-handed. "I'll take my meetings here."

"Don't be ridiculous. I can manage."

"I'm sure you can, but why should you have to when I can help."

"I don't need help."

She pressed her lips together and widened her eyes as she looked around the chaos in the kitchen. "You sure about that?" She chuckled at him and put her hands up in surrender. "I promise not to cook anything. I'll just chop and clean."

Sonny followed her gaze. He met her eyes and sighed. "Your sister, Asha and your dad can just come here. We'll meet in your office. And in between, I'll chop, clean and reorganize the boxes in your office." She raised a hopeful eyebrow at him.

"You really want to tackle those boxes?" A chuckle rumbled from him.

"I really do. You should just give in to me." She took the hair band from her wrist and twined up her hair in a messy bun. "Where are the hair nets and aprons?"

Sonny stopped and stared at her.

"What?"

"You're going off-plan." He smiled at her.

"You're letting someone help you."

He shook his head at her, his lips pressed together,

suppressing a smile as he finally surrendered to her. "Hair nets and aprons are in the closet next to my office."

If there was something more adorable than Sangeeta Parikh in a hair net and apron, he had no idea what it was. Not to mention, she was a pro at chopping.

"Dharm might need to look for a new job. That's amazing," he said as he checked her chopping.

"I used to do the chopping growing up. My mom had help, of course, but I always found it soothing, and it let me spend time with my mom while she cooked. Besides, she always liked it when I chopped, but she was very particular about it. That being said, Dharm is welcome to his job back as soon as he's feeling up to it."

"You like pleasing your mom." Vegetables sizzled as Sonny added them to the tempered spices. His glasses fogged and he turned away from the stove.

"Doesn't everyone?" Sangeeta answered without looking up. Though she didn't sound sure.

"Well, yes. I suppose."

"My mom respects order over chaos." Sangeeta kept chopping potatoes. "Chopping precisely is order."

"It can be a lot. Always trying to be perfect." Sonny went back and gave the okra a stir.

"I wasn't trying to be perfect." Sangeeta's brow furrowed as she continued her task.

"Are you sure?" He nodded at her perfectly diced potatoes as his glasses cleared. He turned back to the stove. It was too easy to get caught up in Sangeeta and lose his cooking focus.

"I did what I wanted."

"Like marrying Param?" Sonny glanced back, but he couldn't see her through the steam on his glasses.

"Like not marrying Param." Sangeeta went silent. "My mother never did like that he was a teacher. She felt there was no money in that." She flushed and focused back on the onions. "She was more impressed by Pandya Hotels."

"Well, the joke is on her. She had no idea that I had nothing to do with Pandya Hotels."

"Except that now, she thinks that she won."

"Is it really about winning and losing, Sangeeta?" He pulled out another pan and heated some oil in it. He tossed in a handful of mustard seeds.

"I want to be my own person." She continued chopping.

"So be your own person." Sonny faced her.

Sangeeta looked up at him as if he said something she'd never heard before. Then she smiled. "How'd you get so smart, Sonny Pandya?"

The mustard seeds started popping and Sonny returned his attention to his stove. They worked in amiable silence. He added more turmeric and chili powder and other spices to the tempering oil, stirring the whole time. He then added the cut potatoes to the pot and gave it a stir.

"What about you?" Sangeeta's voice lifted over the mammoth exhaust fan he had installed.

"What about me?" He had started stuffing samosas while the okra and potatoes cooked.

"You and your parents. You only see them for family dinner."

"I'm being my own person," he half snarked at her.

"But it doesn't have to be at the exclusion of your parents. Reena told me what you want to do with the menu at Lulu's."

"Well, my vision wasn't the one that had counted. When I was there, I wanted to be head chef at Lulu's restaurant. I had plans for that restaurant, for the hotel." He looked around. "Now I have this place, and I can't imagine not doing it." He glanced at her. "Can you grab those onions you chopped?"

She brought them to the stove. He heated another pan and put in oil and mustard seeds and curry leaves. On his say-so, she dumped the onions in and gave it a stir.

"Perfect. Can you do cilantro?"

"Like a pro." She grinned at him and went to the back fridge to get the cilantro.

He watched her go long after she had already gone.

"Your onions will burn if your attention is elsewhere." His mother's voice had him straightening as if he were a child getting caught doing something wrong. "Reminds me of Ba cooking dinner." His mother's voice held no sentiment. She was simply stating fact.

Sonny gave the onions a stir. "Ba was a fabulous cook," he said without turning around. Thinking of his grandmother made him smile. He had learned to cook at her side on his summer trips to India. They had lost her when he was around twelve, but Sonny had already learned the basics from her and had fallen in love with cooking. Looking back, he felt like she had taught him to cook so he could feed his siblings while his parents worked to make them a future in this new country they called home. Nothing got past his grand-mother. It was no coincidence to him that Reena was her spitting image.

Heavy-dress-shoe footsteps came closer behind him, until he felt his mother looking over his shoulder. "Turn off the heat, they'll burn," she instructed as if he were a novice.

Irritated, Sonny turned to face his mother, ignoring her advice. "What's up, Mom? What brings you down here?"

"I can't come to my son's restaurant?" She raised her eyebrows as if she could not imagine why he would ask her that question.

"You can. But you don't." This was her first visit.

She pursed her lips. This was true. "Your father tells me you have a girlfriend."

Sonny held his face in a mask. "Yes." It had been al-most two weeks since the video had gone public.

"You haven't shared this with us." She met his eyes.

"I don't share every detail with you."

"No, just with the internet." She raised an eyebrow.

Sonny's turn to remain silent. The less said the better. His mother had a talent for homing in on weaknesses. It had served her well as a businesswoman. And a mother. "Reena says you are living together."

"That is true." Reena had said only "need-to-know." Mom did not need to know he was in a fake relationship.

"How did you meet her?"

"We met at the beach last year. By accident." Stick with the truth. It's best in a lie.

"Your father said we had arranged a meeting for you both."

Sonny nodded. "You had arranged the meeting through her parents. By the time we met, Sangeeta had already decided to marry someone else."

He had tried to convince his parents to call off the meeting, but they refused. Sangeeta must have tried on her side as well, but to no avail. They had found themselves having coffee together a week after their beach weekend.

"I'm sorry. I tried to get out of this." Sangeeta had *been wide-eyed and sympathetic looking. "But they insisted. Ridiculous, really. Param and I were only 'broken up' for a couple weeks."*

"You're engaged?" Sonny had gone for black coffee, allowing the bitterness to overtake him. Besides, he would never order the chai tea. Tea, tea. Ha!

"Well. After this, yes." Sangeeta played with her cup of coffee, never actually taking a sip of her drink. "Mom won't acknowledge me and Param getting back together, unless I at least meet you."

"You didn't tell her?" So, she had to see him so she could marry someone else. He was a chump.

"What? That we spent three days together at the beach? Hell no. She'd just use that to make marrying Param harder for me."

"She's not a fan of Param's?" He had smirked. That had somehow made him feel much better.

"It's not that she's not a fan of Param's as much as she is a fan of Pandya Hotels." Sangeeta had contin-

ued to spin her coffee cup in her hands. "Did you tell yours?"

Sonny had gulped at his coffee as he shook his head. She didn't need to know that Reena had pestered it out of him while he had moped about. "No. But our parents have something in common, then, at least."

Sangeeta had nodded, knowingly, as children of uber-successful people did know. "Your parents are fans of my grandfather."

"Well, Acharya Inc. is known everywhere, not just India," Sonny had said, the bitter coffee still in his mouth. He glanced at his phone. "We've been here thirty minutes. Coffee's cold. Should satisfy our parents that we gave it shot. Don't you think?"

"Um, yeah. Sure." She had looked at him like she had something to say.

He didn't want to hear it. He stood. There had been so many things he had wanted to say to her. "We could be good together. You make me want to be better. I've never felt as in sync with someone as I did with you at the beach. Don't marry him." He said none of those things. "Good luck to you." He let her go.

"You knew that then, Mom."

"So why are you with her now?" His mother stepped closer and looked up at him and into his eyes. She was trying to catch him in a lie.

Sonny maintained eye contact. There was no room for wavering. "She left him and came to me." It was the truth. Sort of.

"You're not concerned that she might be on a rebound?"

He sighed. "I can take care of myself, Mom."

"I don't want to see you get hurt." At these words, his mother's eyes softened.

Since when? "I won't."

His mother studied him a moment. "Bring her to dinner tomorrow evening. Sunday dinner. Everyone will be there." It was an order, not a request. She started to turn. "Your onions are burned."

Sonny swiveled back to his stove and sure enough, the onions were blackened. He tossed the pan in the sink and turned back, and his mother was gone.

Chapter Nineteen

"So you're the oldest, then Reena, then Jai, who just finished his sophomore year at JMU?" Sangeeta stared straight ahead, her brown eyes focused. He could almost see the family tree she was building in her head. He grinned. Sangeeta definitely did not do anything half-assed.

"That's the easy part. My cousins will be there along with my kaka and my masi."

"I got it." Sangeeta sounded very confidant. Sonny had already learned not to press it when she sounded like this.

He took her hand as they walked up the substantial driveway to his parents' home for the required Sunday dinner his mother had demanded they attend. She intertwined her fingers with his without skipping a beat. As if she wanted to hold his hand. As if they were a real couple. He looked at her as she mentally reviewed the stats he had given her about his family. She was invested in the success of this dinner. Like a real girlfriend. He shook his head of those thoughts. She wasn't his real girlfriend. All of this was for show. To help Reena.

This dinner happened twice a month and both of his parents cooked for it. Which was funny because he had cooked most of their family dinners growing up. The family had expanded over the years, as uncles and aunts immigrated to the States.

"Admit it. Your closet is easier to access now that it is organized." She was smug, but he had to admit, she was right.

He mockingly rolled his eyes. "If you like that whole 'organized vibe' thing, sure."

"You know I do." She laughed. "Though for a guy who doesn't care about plans, you have drilled your family tree into me."

"Well, for a girl who loves a plan, you seem more than willing to wing it." They were at the front door, which was entirely too big.

She rolled her eyes at him. He chuckled. Of course, Sangeeta was not winging it. "If we were a real couple, I'd be doing this too."

Sonny's heart skipped a beat. Was she reading his mind?

"Don't look so panicked. We're not a real couple."

The door opened. "You two going to come in or are you going to stand there making goo-goo eyes at each other in the heat?" Jai pursed his lips, mock disappointment on the young man's face. "Bhai, it's like you have no idea how to treat a woman." He turned to Sangeeta and motioned with his hand for her to enter. "Please come in. It's nice and air-conditioned in here. Allow me to apologize for my idiot brother."

Sangeeta didn't even bother to hide her smirk as she entered. "Thank you."

"I'm Jai, the charming brother."

"Obviously." She laughed. "Nice to meet you, Jai."

Sonny narrowed his eyes at his brother, then smiled. "Get your own girl, squirt." He draped an arm over Sangeeta's shoulders. "This one is mine." If only it were so. What were these thoughts? No. No. No. Sangeeta was not his. And nor should she be. She literally ran from her wedding two weeks ago. He hardly knew her.

Right?

Jai smirked. "We'll see, Bhaiya."

Sonny paused, then let go of Sangeeta and drew his brother in a huge hug. "You're squishing me, Bhaiya."

"That's the point. I missed you."

"Well, if you came home more, you wouldn't have to squish me."

"Damn, Mom has you well trained." Sonny let his brother go.

"I'm a quick study."

"Jai?" His mother's voice carried light and airy from the kitchen.

"Bhaiya's here. And he brought the girl."

Silence. Sangeeta looked him. Sonny gave a slight shake of his head as he inhaled. *Let's do this.*

"Well, bring her back here. And your brother too," his mother called. As if she hadn't demanded Sangeeta's presence.

Jai motioned to her, and she followed his little brother.

Who really wasn't that little anymore. He was as tall as he was. A bit skinnier, but the muscles were there. "You working out, Jai?"

His brother turned around and smiled. "You can tell, huh?"

"I asked didn't I?"

The way his brother's face lit up warmed a part of Sonny that hadn't been happy for a while. He missed the kid. Jai was becoming a man and Sonny was missing it.

He followed Sangeeta and Jai into the kitchen, where his parents were cooking. The aromas were amazing. Reena was still dressed for work, a glass of white wine in her hand. Sunday evening, and she was clearly planning on going back to the office. Sonny would have to talk to her about getting a life. Right now, she was relaxed and laughing at something one of their cousins had said. The football game was on the huge screen mounted over the fireplace. For a family that did not grow up watching TV, his parents certainly had a plethora of them now. A bunch of cousins and his father's sister were crowded in the family room yelling at the TV. They were munching on mixed vegetable pakora and spicy chicken wings.

The kitchen opened to the family room and dining room. It was mild chaos. And he loved it. Sangeeta looked like a deer in headlights. He placed his hand on the small of her back and felt her relax. He whispered to her, "Remember, it's not real. It does not matter what they think of you."

"It's not that." She smiled up at him.

"Sonny! You have been holding out!" His cousin

Neel hugged him, then held out a hand to Sangeeta. "I'm Neel. His favorite cousin. Nice to meet you."

Sangeeta shook Neel's hand. "Nice to meet you too."

"I have to say, Sonny has been very tight-lipped about you."

She looked at Sonny, as if to chide him. "Well, it's been weird."

"A little bit." Neel laughed. "My mom has been all over his dad to find out what's going on." He sipped his beer. "You two getting married or what?"

Sonny shook his head and looked at Sangeeta. "Don't mind Neel. He has no filter."

"Yeah, but she left her wedding—"

"Neel." Sonny glared at his cousin.

"Yeah, okay." He nodded at Sangeeta. "Nice to meet you."

"You too."

Neel walked away and Sonny poured wine for them both.

"He was nice." Sangeeta smiled up at him.

"He was blunt."

"Well... Maybe we should talk about that. Are we getting married?" She brought the wine to her lips, a small smirk and amusement in her eyes. Sonny just stared at her. Being married to Sangeeta would be—no! He would never be married to her, so best to stop thinking about it.

He could see it now. Waking up every morning curled up around her warm body. Having chai together before work. Greeting her in the evening with a fabulous meal. Then going to bed...

"For our story." Sangeeta's words brought him back to reality. "I think we should not address the getting married to anyone, because when we break up, it'll just be more disappointment, you know?" She sipped her wine and continued to look around the room.

"Sounds good." He kept his voice easy, light. He had allowed himself a minute of a fantasy, but now, a hole had been carved into his stomach at the thought of their inevitable breakup.

What had he gotten himself into?

"Ah, there's my son." Jaya Pandya's voice was clear even in the din of the whole family.

"Mom." Sonny turned to face his mother. She untied her apron and set it aside before pulling Sonny into a somewhat awkward embrace.

"You must be the young lady who has made Sonny famous on the internet." His mother turned to her.

"Mom." Sonny's voice was firm. "Meet Sangeeta Parikh. My girlfriend."

"It's nice to meet you, Auntie." Sangeeta extended her hand to his mother and smiled sweetly. Honestly, having Sonny refer to her as his girlfriend gave a pleasing jolt to her body that she had not expected.

Sonny most definitely had his mother's eyes and coloring.

"It's nice to finally meet you as well." His mother shook Sangeeta's hand, taking her in. Her gaze swept Sangeeta's face and landed squarely on her eyes. "My son keeps his private life extremely private, so if not for the internet, I would not even know about you."

Sangeeta glanced at Sonny. His expression had gone hard. She took his hand. His muscles were rigid, but he softened a bit as she leaned into him. She heard him exhale. "Well, things did move very fast. I'm very happy to have been invited here, so I could meet all of you. Sonny talks about his family all the time." Sangeeta embellished a bit.

"Does he, now?" Auntie raised an eyebrow.

"Of course," Sangeeta answered.

"Come, I'll show you the food." Jaya Auntie tucked Sangeeta's hand into her arm and led her toward the kitchen island where the food was. "Your uncle and I have been cooking all day."

Sonny started to follow. "Sunil. Can you make sure everyone has a drink? And refill the chutney bowls, please," his mother said over her shoulder.

"Of course," he mumbled.

Sangeeta looked at Sonny, a mild panic building inside her. Though why she should have any anxiety over this was beyond her. Sonny was right. They were faking. His mother did not have to like her; she only needed to believe them.

Jaya Auntie was gracious enough, showing Sangeeta the various dishes they had made, even making Sangeeta a plate to get her started. Scattered among the Mexican- and Mediterranean-type appetizers were also a few classic Gujrati dishes. She asked questions about Sangeeta's family, which Sangeeta answered truthfully. Sangeeta was just starting to relax when she found that she and Auntie were alone in a small corner of the house on the top floor.

Floor-to-ceiling windows came together at adjacent walls. Built-in bookshelves lined the walls next to windows. A telescope was mounted in the corner in front of the windows, a small stool beside it. A comfy chair and side table were along the bookshelves. The area was part of a loft, with a sofa and another chair, but felt intimate, almost private. Sangeeta had such a place in the house she had grown up in. She suddenly felt nostalgic for that place.

"This is Sonny's area," Auntie said. The older woman's gaze followed her, with laser focus. Her voice had gone from genial host to what Sangeeta could only identify as protective mother.

Sangeeta snapped her gaze to her. "Really?" Sonny had the same type of oasis that she did. They had more of a connection than she had thought. She also had the floor-to-ceiling bookshelves, but instead of the telescope, she had a desk where she did all her planning. She kept a smaller version in the apartment she shared with Param. But it wasn't quite the same as her space in the Mumbai house. She had always entered that space with coffee and a light heart. Though now, she would prefer Sonny's chai.

"He didn't tell you of his love of the stars?" Auntie sounded shocked, but almost as if she'd just had a suspicion confirmed.

"He did. He did not tell me about this little area." Sangeeta walked along the bookshelves. No surprise, the majority of books were either about astronomy or cooking. She felt closer to him as she imagined him sitting on the stool and looking to the stars or reading about them in the comfy chair while he drank his chai. Maybe he came up with new recipes as well.

"Why are you with him?" Auntie's voice left no room for interpretation. It was clear what she was asking.

There was only one acceptable answer.

She turned and looked at Auntie, a smile on her face. "Because I love him." Huh. It was easier to say than she'd have thought. She must be getting good at this acting thing.

Auntie's eyes shot up, nearly into her forehead. "Is that so? Were you not poised to marry some other man just two weeks ago?"

Sangeeta nodded. "Yes. But marrying Param would have been a mistake. I simply did not realize it until the moment I was to marry him."

"Your parents must be beside themselves."

"They are." Sangeeta pressed her lips together.

"My son likes to fix people. He likes to help people. It's what makes him a wonderful person, easy to love." Jaya Auntie fixed Sangeeta in her gaze. Her voice was soft but commanding. There was a purpose to this. Here, her voice hardened. "Let me be clear and up front with you, Sangeeta. I am no fool. You seem to be a lovely young woman, but you also have some issues. It's not that I cannot see what my son sees in you. In fact, it is all too apparent what he sees in you. He sees someone who needs fixing. You, my dear, are broken in his eyes, and he wants to fix you. This does not mean that he loves you."

Sangeeta felt the blood drain from her. She was slightly light-headed, though her logic could not understand why. Why did she feel like the ground under her had collapsed?

Why did it feel like her heart had broken?

She should be relieved. She and Sonny were not really in love. There was no intention on either of their parts to stay together for real. His mother had just handed her a great breakup excuse.

She gripped the back of the chair to steady herself. Though her emotions swirled like a tornado through her, her response came without thought. "I'm afraid you are mistaken. It may be unconventional, but we *are* in love. We are very much together." She defended their relationship as if it were real.

"Hey. Everyone is waiting on you to start dinner." Sonny walked up the steps just then. He looked from his mother to Sangeeta and back. "What's going on?"

Neither woman spoke. Sonny turned to his mother. "Mom?"

"I'm just making sure everyone understands how things are." She was completely unapologetic.

"How things are is that Sangeeta and I are in love... with each other." Sonny came and stood by Sangeeta's side. "We are together."

Sangeeta warmed at the ease with which Sonny declared his "love" for her, then immediately reprimanded herself for it. This was fake, which was a good thing, because no way was she ready for a relationship.

"Of course." Jaya Auntie flicked her gaze between them. "I'll just go down and get things started." She brushed past them without another word or glance.

Sonny immediately spun to face Sangeeta. "What happened?" He put his hands on her shoulders and inspected her face, drawing his gaze over her as if checking for any physical harm. "You okay? What did she say to you?"

Sangeeta clasped his hands in hers. "I'm fine." She

nodded at him when he looked at her. "She's just being a mom. Looking out for you. Making sure I'm for real."

"And? Did you convince her?"

Sangeeta nodded, forcing a smile onto her face. "Well, she's not fond of me, so yes. I do believe that she thinks we are together."

Sonny took Sangeeta's hand. "Mom's a trial-by-fire kind of person. Whatever she said to you is of no consequence. Trust me."

Sangeeta shrugged. "Of course. And what does it matter anyway? We're not really together."

Sonny nodded. "Right."

They both went down to join the family for dinner.

"So how do you like being a wedding planner?" his father asked while they ate together.

"I love it." Sangeeta lit up when she talked about her work.

"Must be hard, though," piped up Neel, "having run from your own wedding, to get clients."

Sangeeta shot Sonny a look. "Oh. Well. Luckily, people forget," she said. There was silence as Neel continued to eat, oblivious of what he had just said.

"Well, beti," his mother said, "lucky that Asha Gupta decided to use you when she needed a change."

"Very lucky. Though I owe it to Reena." Sangeeta nodded at Reena. "She introduced us."

Sonny's father looked from Sangeeta to Reena. "Did she?"

Reena simply looked at their father with a blank face and kept eating.

Sonny and Sangeeta passed an enjoyable afternoon

with his cousins. Sangeeta did not know anything about football, but she was a quick study under his foi's tutelage. Before he knew it, she was shouting at the TV alongside that aunt and his cousins.

The game ended, the signal that it was time to go home. Sonny and Jai had done the dishes, and now Sonny was drying his hands as everyone said their goodbyes. He leaned against the granite counter next to his little brother and watched. Jai had something to say about each and every member of the family. His observations were funny, accurate and loving. Sonny hadn't laughed this hard in a long while. He watched Sangeeta with the family. She was engaged and genuine and real.

She glanced his way and caught him looking and it took him a beat too long to look away.

"Damn, Bhaiya. You got it bad." Jai was shaking his head at him.

"What? No, I don't." He couldn't.

Jai's eyes widened. "Are you kidding me? The way you two just looked at each other, it was like—"

Sangeeta walked up just then. Sonny straightened and folded the towel, throwing his brother a warning look. "Ready to go?"

"Yeah. Sure."

She turned to Jai. "I'm glad to finally have met you."

"Me too." He wrapped his arms around Sangeeta in huge bear hug, which she returned.

Sonny ignored the pang of guilt. They were lying to this young man.

"And thanks for letting us use your appointment time

with the telescope the other day. It was incredible!"
Sangeeta gushed.

"You two," Reena whispered to him as she nodded
at Sangeeta. "Meet me outside."

"Bye!" Reena called out to their parents. "See you
at the office tomorrow!"

Everyone else was gone. Jai gave Sonny a huge bear
hug and headed out with some friends. His parents were
sitting next to each other on the sofa, each holding a
glass of wine. They clinked glasses and sipped, and his
mother rested her head on his father's shoulder.

Sangeeta sighed. "My parents are the exact same."

Sonny raised his eyebrows.

"Opposites attract, what can I say?" she whispered.
"You'll see. Next weekend."

"Bye, Mom. Dad," Sonny called.

"Drive safe." They turned their heads from the sofa
to watch them walk out.

"Will do."

Sonny took her hand as they exited the house. It
was such a natural move. Reena was waiting for them
by his car.

"You two need to do more stuff together. Asha is getting antsy for content." Reena spoke in hushed tones.

"Reena." His was weary. "Can we do this later? Tomorrow is my day off and I'm going hiking."

"And I have wedding stuff to do. I just got another
big client," Sangeeta added.

Sonny turned to her. "Yeah? That's great, Sangeeta."
He squeezed her hand. "Who is it?"

Before Sangeeta could answer, Reena waved her
hands. "That's perfect. You can both go hiking. Take

pictures. Post. Like real couples." She glanced at her phone and bolted for her car. "I'm late. Good plan!"

"Who are you meeting at 10:00 p.m. on a Sunday night?" Sonny called after his sister.

"Potential client." Reena was in her car before either of them could say anymore.

Chapter Twenty

Sonny was awake before dawn. If you can call it awake when you hardly slept. It was going to be a long two months if he could not find a way to get some sleep with Sangeeta in the apartment.

Sangeeta was already dressed, coffee brewing, when he stumbled out of the bathroom.

"I hope that is not indicative of how the day is going to go." She smirked at him.

"I'll be fine."

"You don't look fine."

He glared at her. She seemed to have no trouble sleeping. Meanwhile, thoughts of her haunted him all night, keeping him awake. She appeared to not be plagued in that way at all. He inhaled deeply. The aroma of coffee was almost as calming as that of chai. But not quite. "I'll take some of that though."

"It was faster than chai. And my chai sucks." Sangeeta handed him a mug as she sipped hers. "I mapped out a plan for hitting the trails. The weather is going to turn on us in the afternoon, but if we stick with this—" she turned her phone to him "—we'll be able to catch the main vistas before the torrential downpour. Also, I found your extra water bladder. I hope you don't mind if I use it."

He sipped the coffee. It was fantastic, as far as coffee went. "What did you do to the coffee?"

"Cinnamon."

He nodded his approval and locked the idea away for future use. "We don't need a plan for a hike. We just hike. We take water, snacks, first aid kit. Follow the path."

"But you could get stuck in the wrong place when it rains." Her brow furrowed.

He waved a dismissive hand at her. "Live a little, Sangeeta. It's just rain."

"But—"

"It'll be fine." He finished his coffee, feeling much more awake. "Give me a minute to dress."

He quickly changed, skipped the shave and grabbed his hiking pack and water bladder. "Let's do this," he grumbled. He preferred hiking alone. It gave him time to center himself for the week. It was cute that she had a plan. But a plan was not needed for hiking. Hiking was meant to be spontaneous.

Sangeeta grabbed his keys. "I'll drive. I already mapped out the perfect place to park."

"I already know the best route and where to park. I go every week." He held out his hands for the keys. "Besides. Nobody drives Buck but me."

"Buck?" She quirked that challenging smile that he was starting to love. No. He didn't *love* her smile, he *liked* her smile. She was, after all an extremely attractive woman. Who happened to have a very nice smile. With dimples.

"Yeah. What of it?"

"Nothing. But 'Buck' is getting a new driver today."

An hour and a half later, Sangeeta gently shook him awake. He must have passed out as soon as she started driving. It was the best sleep he'd had in weeks. "Hey. We're here. We're parking closer to the trailhead, in case we get caught in the storm."

Sonny got out of the car, surprisingly refreshed, and squinted into the sun as he donned his baseball cap and sunglasses. Clear blue skies, and a bright sun rising. The air was typical June in Maryland, warm, moist, promising high humidity and heat. The one thing that was not promised was a storm.

"I think your weather app is wrong," he grunted.

Sangeeta shook her head. She too had donned a baseball cap, pulling her ponytail through the hole in the back. He loved her hair, but when it was pushed away like this, he could enjoy the curve of her neck and jawline. He started to reach out to touch her.

"What?" She pulled back.

"Oh, uh…nothing. Bug." He waved his hand as if a bug had been on her. He was officially an idiot.

"Bugs are part of hiking. I'm okay with that." She sneered at him. "Anyway, I know it seems like there won't be, but there is definitely going to be a summer storm."

Sonny shook his head. "Whatever." They walked a bit to the trailhead.

Sangeeta pulled out her phone. "We should take a selfie here. At the trailhead." Sangeeta held out her phone, they both looked into the lens and she took the photo. Sangeeta started walking, Sonny followed. "I usually take a different route."

"Well, try this today."

He sighed. She was messing with his hike and his peace of mind. He followed her and they walked in silence for a bit.

"So, whatever happened between you and your dad?" Sangeeta dropped the question casually, but there was nothing casual about it.

He stared at her. Not only did he have to share his hike with her, she wanted to talk about his dad? "I'd rather not talk about it."

She shrugged as if she didn't care, but not before Sonny caught the downturn of her mouth. He couldn't see her eyes, but he imagined the disappointment that was there. He grunted and took the lead.

"Um. We need to go the other way, so we don't get caught in the—"

"Look at the sky, Sangeeta. There are no clouds in the sky. In fact, the sun is getting ready to scorch us. The storm is not coming."

"Yes. It is." She was firm.

"No. It isn't. The app can be wrong." He continued his chosen path forward. She sighed but followed.

They stopped every so often to take a photo to post, each time smiling into the camera as if they were just the happiest couple in love.

"I don't like talking about whatever is happening between me and my dad," Sonny let out.

Sangeeta shrugged. "Sure. I get it. I don't like talking about my mom and me."

They made it up to a vista. It was no more than a clearing that allowed an incredible view of the sky, the hills and the town below.

Sangeeta opened her bag and pulled out a couple of peanut butter and jelly sandwiches. She handed him one. Sonny pulled out a bag of chips from his pack. Her eyes lit up. "Oh! I couldn't find any in the kitchen."

"I keep a stash in the hall closet." He opened the bag and held it out to her. She took a few, and he took a handful and proceeded to put them inside his sandwich. He glanced at her. She was engrossed in doing the same thing. She glanced at him, then broke out into a huge smile. "Great minds think alike."

He shrugged but continued what he was doing. But he could not suppress the smile that came across his face. Just as he took the first bite of his sandwich, a shadow fell across them. He looked up. Sure enough, a huge dark storm cloud had materialized from nowhere. Sangeeta had already shoved her sandwich back in her bag and was standing, looking for a place to attempt to keep dry.

"Time to move," she said.

There was nowhere to go. They pulled on their rain jackets and started down the mountain. They had hardly taken ten steps when the rain started to fall. It fell in large drops, fast and hard. Within minutes, they were both soaked to the skin. Sonny followed Sangeeta, as the water on his sunglasses impeded his vision. Besides, she seemed to know where she was going. After what seemed forever, in a downpour, Sonny caught blurry sight of the canopy as Sangeeta led them to it.

They ducked under the very small shelter and removed their hoods and hats.

"I told you it would rain." She was irritatingly not smug about it.

"Lucky this canopy was here."

"Luck? Luck had nothing to do with it. I knew it was here," Sangeeta said as she removed her hat and sunglasses.

Water dripped from her hairline down her face. Her rain jacket stuck to her body, hugging her curves in all the right places. Sonny forced himself to look away from her.

"You knew it was here? I've never seen it before." Sonny looked around. He didn't usually come this way.

"Planning." This, she was smug about.

Sonny said nothing.

The rain slowed down but did not stop. There was a small bench under the small roof and Sangeeta sat down on it, making room for him. When he sat, their legs touched. Her skin was cool from the water.

They sat in silence as the rain fell in sheets before them, cooling the air from the sweltering sun.

Sonny watched Sangeeta as she stared out at the rain. "It's kind of soothing," she said softly.

"It is," he said, still looking at her.

She turned to face him. There was doubt in her eyes. He grinned and turned to watch the rain fall. Water dripped down his face. His clothes were stuck to him, as hers were to her. He ran his fingers back through his hair to get it out of his eyes. He glanced at her, and she watched him. He looked back at the rain.

"I started out washing dishes for the restaurant in Lulu's, when I was in high school." He spoke softly. "The hotel and restaurant were smaller then. They expanded while I was in culinary school. I used to work whenever I had the chance at the restaurant. The chef at the time would let me chop things, give me pointers. By the time I graduated, business was starting to slow down a bit. People were going for more casual fare. Restaurants like ours were reserved for special occasions. I started on the line, at the bottom, then quickly worked my way up to sous chef. I was in line for head chef. When the head chef retired, he told my father I was ready to take over, so I did.

"I wanted to change the menu—not completely, but I wanted to add Indian food—Indian street food—during the day at first, keeping the dinner menu intact. Then I wanted to offer Indian food at dinner. My father was all about fitting in with what the expected notion of haute cuisine was. I wanted our culture to be on the menu. Simple, fun street foods, belly-filling comfort foods. Once I became head chef, I started with street food at lunch. A couple weeks after I started, I came in to find Kiren Mistry in my job." Anger flooded through him at the thought of Kiren. "Kiren and I had gone head-to-head on everything in culinary school. Ask Amar, he'll tell you."

"So, your father not only replaced you without your knowledge, but he hired your nemesis." Sangeeta sounded amused.

"Basically, yes." Sonny nodded. "Is that funny?"

"No. It's something my mom would do." She chuckled. "That's why you don't cook for that hotel?"

"Yep."

Sangeeta shrugged. "Well, now you have a chance to make it on your own."

"Except that I'm cooking for Asha's wedding. I have already gotten new customers. I have a sweet sixteen in a couple weeks, and a few birthday parties. Not to mention more people at the restaurant."

"These are all good things." Sangeeta laid a hand on his forearm.

"But I got those things because I am cooking for that hotel."

"So what? You're doing all the work. It's your menu. And your sister said Kiren left."

Reena had mentioned that, but it was now striking him that he never asked who the head chef was over there.

"Did you ever confront your dad?" Sangeeta's hand on his arm was almost burning a hole through his thin rain jacket.

"For what? It's his hotel. He can do what he wants with it."

"Does he even know why you quit?" Sangeeta challenged him.

"Isn't it obvious?"

"It's obvious to you. Maybe not him. He did come down to the restaurant to see you."

"Because of that video. Because of you. He's gloating because he introduced us, and now he gets to be right." Sonny shook his head, his anger and sadness returning. This was why he didn't discuss this.

"Except that he's not really right." Sangeeta grinned. "Because we aren't really together, now, are we?"

"No. I guess we are not." Though it struck him in that moment that he'd rather be wrong about that.

"The sun's out and the rain is stopping." Sangeeta stood and took off her rain jacket. Sonny stared at her. Her T-shirt and shorts clung to every curve in her body. He could not tear his gaze away. He did not want to. He'd never envied a T-shirt before.

"What are you looking at?" she narrowed her eyes at him.

"What?" He snapped out his reverie and took off his rain jacket as well, trying not to look at her. "Nothing…it's just…the rain… and the—" He was babbling.

"Uh-huh." A small smile started on her face as she ran her gaze over him and his wet clothes. "Rain."

"We…uh." He swallowed hard. "We need to dry off. Maybe on the way down."

Sangeeta grinned. "Follow me."

Not about to argue with her anymore, Sonny waved his arm out for her to lead the way. Sangeeta led them down the sunniest paths, and soon enough they were both fairly dry.

"Come this way." Sonny veered off the path into some high grass.

"But it's off the path." Sangeeta furrowed her brow. "It may not be safe."

"I've been here many times." He met her eyes. "Trust me." He held out his hand.

She searched his face for a moment as if contemplating him. Then she took his hand and followed him. *She trusted him.* Sonny led them through some brush and over felled trees before they waded through mud puddles.

"Squishy." Sangeeta giggled. "This is definitely not on the map."

"I know." He chuckled.

Sonny held on to her hand and led her to a clearing that opened to a small waterfall.

Sangeeta gasped. "It's an oasis." She squeezed his hand. "This is beautiful." She let go of his hand to touch the water. She looked around for a few minutes, taking it in. Then she turned to him. "This place. This is why you come here every week."

He nodded.

"Do you always come alone?"

"Until today." He gave a crooked smile. He was no longer irritated by her presence. "Sometimes I bring a tent and sleeping bag and camp out. Under the stars." He glanced up. "Not a lot of light pollution up here."

"Must be beautiful for viewing," she said, still taking in the surroundings. "Like the beach," she nearly whispered, but he heard her.

"Yeah. Like the beach," he whispered back, as if by whispering, they were somehow keeping that time in the past. He watched her as she took in the beauty of the area.

"What did my mom say to you?" he finally asked. "You seemed…off after that conversation."

Sangeeta tensed ever so slightly, but he noticed. She frowned and shook her head. "Nothing your fake girlfriend can't handle."

He nodded. Fake girlfriend. He kept forgetting that she was going to move on in less than a couple of months, that she had in fact only recently left her fiancé in the mandap. He knew this. He knew this in his head.

Someone should tell his heart.

Chapter Twenty-One

Sonny turned his gaze away from her and found a relatively dry, flat boulder for them to sit on. He patted the space next to him and she sat down, bringing her knees to her chest. The waterfall crashed softly into the lake below it, adding to the quiet sounds of chirping and wind that was their soundtrack.

She could no longer see what was in his eyes as his glasses had darkened to sunglasses. His mother had not been messing around. The more Sangeeta looked around her, the more she saw that Jaya Auntie was correct.

Sonny was doing all this faking just to fix things for his sister. He had promised Jai more of whatever little time he had. It only made sense that any affection he might have for her was related to her having run from Param. He had taken care of her injured foot. Then fed her. Gave her a place to stay. He had even carried her that night when her feet hurt. Sonny Pandya was a helper, a fixer. He was just doing what came naturally to him. It didn't mean that he had *feelings* for her. Therefore, the logical thing would be to squash any real feelings for him she may have been experiencing.

"So... What's the deal with you and your mom?" Sonny asked quietly, bumping his shoulder to hers.

Sangeeta thrilled at the small touch. "She's just... She has high expectations."

"Don't all parents?"

Sangeeta nodded. "I just learned when I was little that if I stayed on script, she was never disappointed in me. My script said that by the time I was twenty-six, I needed to be married, so I could have my first child at twenty-eight, my second at thirty and third at thirty-two. I needed to have *this* job, so by the time I had my second child, I could open my own wedding planning company, and eventually become exclusive." Sangeeta looked at Sonny. He was looking at her, attentive. The sun had dried them, so sadly his T-shirt was no longer clinging to what had turned out to be some very impressive muscles that were always hidden behind chef's whites. He had been looking at her, wet clothes clinging to her, but Sangeeta was not about to investigate that.

She squinted, as if the sun were in her eyes, but the reality was it was very intense, sitting here with him, talking about her family.

"Param fit my plan." She paused, still facing the sun to buy a minute as she turned to him. "Sonny, I... The truth is that I was not faking at the beach. That was *me*." She sighed. "You, simply, were not part of my plan.

When Param wanted to get back together, I jumped at that chance to get back on track. To get back on plan. It's what I knew. It's what was—comfortable, predictable. That was all that mattered. It was selfish… I don't expect you to understand, but I want you to know that I am sorry."

Sonny stared out at the waterfall. Damn those sunglasses, she couldn't read him.

"So you are the planner extraordinaire because you're trying to please your mom?" He continued as if she hadn't said anything about the beach.

"It started out that way, but then it just became…who I was. Who I am." Sangeeta shrugged.

"What happens if you go off-plan?"

Sangeeta sighed. "I end up soaking wet in the hills, next to a stream with a chef."

Sonny chuckled and nodded.

"Why did you run, Sangeeta?" His voice was quiet, unobtrusive.

Sangeeta stared out at the water. "As I stood in front of those double doors waiting for them to be opened, the life I would've had with Param flashed before me. Marriage, career, children, families." She looked down, then back at the water. "It was a nice life, no doubt about it. But, something was missing. I didn't know what. I still do not, but every cell in my body knew something was off. So, I ran."

Sonny was sitting shoulder to shoulder with her. She felt him turn his head to her, his breath on her ear. "What kind of life do you see for yourself now?"

Sangeeta turned to face him. He had removed his glasses, and her face was mere inches from his. Something electric passed between them. Her gaze swept his mouth and she considered what it might be like to let herself go and press her lips against his. Today, here in the rain, in this place, with Sonny looking at her with what could only be desire, smelling like rain and earth, it seemed the most natural thing to do. She moved a millimeter closer to him.

"Sangeeta, I..." He caught her eye and moved closer, the air between their lips charged with the possibility of this kiss. He met her eyes, silently asking permission. She was about to give it when she remembered his mother's warning and she froze. Sonny was just trying to fix her. He couldn't possibly have feelings for her, any more than her feelings for him could be real. Kissing him was simply giving in to her hormones. So what, the little devil on her shoulder said. Kissing did not have to involve emotions. She leaned a bit closer. But what about her emotions? the devil on her other shoulder said. Kissing Sonny right now would only serve to give her more of the feels. She couldn't afford that.

Thunder boomed above and rain fell again on them in sheets.

They popped up. Sonny wrapped his rain jacket around her followed by his arm as he guided them back to the main path. They found the main path with ease and continued down, while the rain soaked them through again. Sangeeta tried not to stare as Sonny's T-shirt once again clung to him, putting on display the muscles in his strong back and shoulders. Perfect for leaning on. She shook her head and dismissed those thoughts. She would not be leaning on him for anything. Param's wounded eyes flashed before her. She could never forgive herself if she put the same pain in Sonny's eyes.

No. They would finish this charade and then go their separate ways.

He gripped her hand as they descended the trail together. The rain let up just as they arrived at the car soaked and muddy.

Sonny unlocked the car and she opened the trunk, pulling out a second backpack. From this she pulled out two towels and handed one to Sonny.

"You brought towels? I thought your plan avoided getting wet."

"I have to be prepared for the wild card," she said as she attempted to dry herself.

"The rain?"

"No." She shook her head. "You."

Chapter Twenty-Two

Sangeeta passed a couple of days in her office at Lu-lu's Boutique Hotel. She left early and returned late to avoid seeing too much of Sonny. The fact that she had almost kissed him while hiking unsettled her. She had no solid plan right now, but kissing Sonny Pandya was definitely not on it.

The truth was that she had hurt someone when she had a plan, so what was the guarantee that she wouldn't hurt someone if she had none?

Besides, the Parikh family dinner was tonight. A mid-week dinner was not ideal, but her mother was getting impatient. She glanced at Seema Masi's house from the street where Sonny had parked. *Mansion* was a more appropriate word. It was where her parents came when they were Stateside. She was bringing Sonny into the den.

There were a few cars in the circular driveway already. She recognized Nikhil's car, so of course Anita was here. She had only texted Anita in response to her phone calls, to avoid that confrontation. Tina and Jake's car was right behind Nikhil's. Her brother Hiral's car was there. The house was so big, Rocky and Easha and their new baby lived in one wing of it. Great. Full house. She turned in her seat to Sonny.

"Okay." She kept her voice matter-of-fact and professional, like she did with clients. "Full house, but not as full as yours, so more time for scrutiny. Not to mention, ninety-five percent of the people in that house are lawyers."

Sonny nodded with a grin that said "bring it." "So nowhere safe?"

She sighed and looked out the window again. "Dada. My grandfather is safe." But he was the last person she wanted to fool. "Let's just get it over with." She opened the car door and got out, the heat and humidity hitting her like a thick wet wall. Sonny was at her side almost instantly. Must be those long legs. He held out his hand for her to take.

She rolled her eyes as if it were a chore to take his hand, but the truth was, she had missed holding his hand all week. This was a legit reason to interlace her fingers with his, so she took it. His fingers were strong, his grip gentle, and it felt like the most natural thing to do.

"Got to make it look good," she said as she came up next to him, her fingers threaded with his.

He looked amazing today. Simple light blue button-down shirt and jeans, thick hair shaved close on the sides and brushed to the side on top. Dark-rimmed glasses. Clean-shaven. Full lips. *Stop.* She drew her gaze slowly away from him, but not before she noted that he rolled up the sleeves of that shirt, revealing those forearms built from handling pots and pans. She'd felt the hard strength of those muscles on the hike when she'd casually laid her hand on his forearm as they chatted. "Yeah. We do." He squeezed her hand and smiled down at her. "Ready?"

She nodded and they approached the large double doors that were similar to the ones at her mother's house in India. Before she could knock, the door opened, and Tina stood there with one hip jutted out, her hair in a sleek ponytail, almost no make-up on her brown skin.

"Just wanted to give you a heads-up—the two sisters are acting weird."

"What do you mean?" Sangeeta asked. Her mother and her masi loved each other, but they usually got on each other's nerves when they were in the same country.

"I mean they're being—nice." Tina scowled her disbelief. "To each other."

Sangeeta shook her head. "Unbelievable." If they were getting along, something was up. She just hoped it wasn't her. "Is Jake here?"

"Getting drinks." Tina smirked at them.

"He's a good man, Tina." Sangeeta stepped into the house, still holding Sonny's hand. Tina's gaze flitted over their hands, before making eye contact with Sonny. "Welcome to the jungle."

That the kitchen is the heart of the home is true in any house, but it was especially true in the Joshi household, more so in the last year or so. Seema Masi had become a grandmother, courtesy of her oldest son, Rocky, and his wife, Easha. She had also slowly let go of the reins at the law firm she and her late husband had built. Rocky ran most of the day-to-day with the help of competent assistants. His daughter, Karina, was the sheer apple of everyone's eye, with all family members vying for a chance to hold her.

It was this that Sangeeta and Sonny walked into. Seema Masi and Neepa were busy doting on little Karina, who could sit up and smile with such charm, she had her tough-as-nails grandmothers eating out of her hand. Tina walked in behind them. Though no one said a word, everyone stopped to look at them. The room fell silent as she and Sonny walked in, still hand in hand. Her brother, Hiral, nodded at her, his lips smashed tight against each other. His new wife, Meeta, offered her a nod, but her expression was one of confusion. Rocky and Easha just watched her. Nikhil looked sympathetic. Anita's jaw dropped open. Neepa picked up Karina as she studied Sangeeta. Her masi glanced at her sister, before turning questioning eyes on Sangeeta. Her father stood in the back, quietly assessing her. Even Jake had stopped pouring drinks to look at them.

Sangeeta leaned toward Sonny. It was an instinct really. She hardly knew she was doing it until she felt Sonny gently squeeze her hand. She inhaled as she scanned the room, trying to decide whom to address first. Baby Karina seemed the safest bet.

"Sangeeta, beti." Her grandfather's voice boomed from behind everyone.

Sangeeta turned to her grandfather, exhaling relief as tears of gratitude filled her eyes. "Dada!"

"Come, give me a hug." He opened his arms to her,

and it was all Sangeeta could do to not run to the sanctuary he offered.

She had to cross the room to reach him, but that meant leaving Sonny to the wolves as it were. He loosened his grip on her hand to let her go. She dropped his hand and went to her grandfather. Dada wrapped her in his arms and his familiar, comforting scent.

"Don't let them get to you," he whispered. "Just tell them." He pulled back and looked her in the eye. "Tell them the truth."

She dropped his gaze and turned back to see Sonny still standing there, her family unsure of what to do. She returned to Sonny's side, her hand at her side. She stretched her fingers, and Sonny's fingers instantly entwined with hers.

"Okay everyone," she started. "I ran from my wedding. It wasn't planned. I just…" She found Anita's eyes. "I just couldn't marry Param. I am sorry that I did not come to that conclusion sooner, to save everyone the cost and work and time that went into planning the wedding. It's been over two weeks since then. I know we haven't talked." She glanced around the room. "What do you want to know?"

Another pin-drop silence, then her brother spoke. "Are you happy?"

Sangeeta squeezed Sonny's hand and looked at him. A smile, a real smile came over her face. "Yes." She turned back to her family. "Yes. I am." And in that moment, she found that she really was. "This is Sonny. Sonny Pandya."

"Isn't that who Mom—" started her brother.

"Yes," Sonny said. "Our parents did try to set us up

some time ago. We weren't ready at the time. Now, we're in a better spot." He grinned at her. "Sometimes, our parents are right."

A deep laughter resounded. Rocky was laughing. "I call BS." He shook his head. "No way Sangeeta runs from her wedding to be with you. No offense, I'm sure you're fabulous. But Sangeeta needs a plan. It's what makes her—Sangeeta."

Sangeeta wasn't sure if she was more offended that Rocky did not believe her, or that he said that she was nothing without her plans. She opened her mouth, but Sonny spoke first. "Rocky, is it?"

Rocky nodded.

"Sangeeta is plenty more than just her plans. She's smart, she's funny, she's determined and extremely caring. Sure, she likes a good, detailed plan, and sometimes that's exactly what we need." His voice went soft and he looked at her. "But sometimes—" he shrugged "—we don't. We take a risk and see what happens."

A warm flush rose to her face.

"The point is, she's infinitely more than her plans." It seemed like Sonny had forgotten that there were other people around. It was just the two of them here. "She's amazing."

Sangeeta was locked into his gaze, unable to tear herself away. Her heart raced. What was he saying? He couldn't possibly mean what he was saying.

But what if he did?

"This man has been in this house for ten minutes, with you all judging him and Sangeeta." Nikhil broke the spell. "At least give the man a drink." Nikhil moved to the bar, to help Jake pour drinks. Easha took little

Karina from her Masi Ba, and came to greet them, as light chatter returned to the room.

"Ooh, let me see my girl!" Sangeeta held her hands out. "She grew a lot in a few weeks." Easha moved in close to hand her the baby. "He's cute," she whispered.

Sangeeta pulled Karina close and glanced behind her at Sonny, who was sipping a beer as he talked to Nikhil. He really was. She smiled at her cousin-sister-in-law in gratitude.

"No, I'm serious. Super-hot guy. Param was handsome for sure, but you two, you look good together. Like you belong together. Your feelings for each other are obvious," Easha Bhabi stated quite firmly as she continued to assess Sonny.

"Hey, stop hogging my favorite cousin, Bhabs." Nikhil handed Sangeeta a glass of her favorite white summer wine.

Sangeeta took the wine and hugged her cousin. "Thanks."

"Anything for my little sister." He squeezed her tight.

"Hey, Sangeeta." Anita came up behind Nikhil. "Sonny."

Sonny dipped his chin at her. "Anita."

"Um… Sonny, I just want to apologize—" Anita started.

Sonny shook his head. "Your brother set us up on one date, over a year ago." He looked at Sangeeta, meeting her eyes. "Clearly we were both meant for other things."

Sangeeta froze as he looked at her. What she saw there made her ridiculously happy. There seemed to be genuine feeling in his words and his eyes. His mother's warning sounded in her brain. Karina chose that time to squawk and the moment was gone.

Sonny turned back to Anita. She was grinning. "Clearly," she said softly. "At least we'll have a story to tell our kids that will totally gross them out." She turned to Sangeeta. "Though you and I are going to talk about why you never said anything to me." Anita tried to look stern, but Sangeeta saw the love in there.

Sonny laughed and raised his glass to Anita. She clinked her wine with his bottle. "To family, then."

Sonny did not miss a beat. He met Sangeeta's eyes and nodded at Nikhil and Anita. "To family."

Anita was going to kill her when she found out the truth.

Karina chose that moment to lunge toward Sonny. "Oh!" Sangeeta exclaimed as she placed a securing hand on the baby's belly. "I think she wants you."

"About time." He grinned as he set down his beer and reached for the baby, who had stretched out her arms to him.

Karina practically jumped out of her arms to him, where she settled in quite nicely against Sonny's chest, as if she had nowhere else to go. Lucky baby.

What? She needed to get a grip.

"Well, we have a baby whisperer in our midst." Rocky came up, raising his glass to Sonny. "Now I know who to turn to for babysitting." He reached around and gave Sangeeta a hug. "Hi, little sister, how are you?" he whispered, his voice laced with concern.

She returned the hug. "I'm okay. Really."

Rocky pulled back, his brow furrowed as he studied her face for signs of trouble in her. After a moment, he gave her a tight smile. "Okay. But if you need anything, *anything*, you know we're here for you."

Sangeeta nodded, afraid to speak. Although at this moment, the truth about Sonny was getting quite hazy. Better check her feelings before someone got hurt.

"I remember when Sangeeta was that little." Her brother, Hiral, and Meeta Bhabi joined the group.

"No way, Bhaiya." Sangeeta smiled at him. "You were like four when I was that old." Hiral came over and gave her a hug. "Doesn't mean I don't remember." He squeezed her for a second or two longer than was completely necessary. He pulled back and studied her.

"You sure you're okay?" He waved the nose of his beer bottle between her and Sonny. "Because no one else is saying it, but this—" he looked pointedly at Sonny "—is weird."

"I know it seems that way, Bhaiya. But honestly—" she found herself smiling in Sonny's direction "—it's not that weird. Not to me."

Hiral kept his arm draped over her shoulder, and she leaned into it as she watched Sonny chatting with Easha Bhabi and Meeta Bhabi, an extremely calm Karina relaxing in his arms. Contentment like she had not experienced flooded through her.

Sonny pushed up his glasses as he slightly bounced while holding the baby. He was laughing and nodding at something Meeta Bhabi said. He turned toward Sangeeta and caught her watching him, but she could not look away. He smiled at her, before returning to her sisters-in-law, and something electric flooded through her.

Sangeeta continued to watch him only because she found it impossible to look away. She could have lived in that moment forever. There was no past, no future, just *now*. She could not remember a time when she had lived so fully in the present.

"Damn, girl. You haven't looked at anyone like that ever," Hiral said softly. "Not even Param."

That was not possible, was it? She was going to marry Param. She didn't though, did she? But that didn't mean she was having real feelings for Sonny. Sure, she had feelings. But one could have feelings of affection for a good friend. Sonny was certainly that. After the past couple of weeks living and working together, they were bound to have developed a friendship, even a fondness for one another. It was normal what she was feeling. They were friends. Good friends, even. Sangeeta downed her wine. She regretted her empty glass in the next moment as her mother finally made her way over to her.

"Beti. How are you?" Her mother cut her eyes to Sonny.

Hiral released her, but met her eyes. She nodded that she was fine. He patted her shoulder and stepped a few feet away. Sangeeta turned to face her mother, keeping her back to Sonny. No need to get caught looking at him. "I'm good, Mom."

Her mother scanned her face, looking for signs of what? Sangeeta had no idea. Deception? No that was Sangeeta's own guilt talking. Her father came up behind Neepa and placed a hand on her shoulder. Sangeeta watched what she had seen so many times before, growing up. Her mother probably didn't even realize she was doing it, but she leaned ever so slightly into that hand and back into her father, as if, if he were standing next to her, there should not be any space between them. That small act of closeness had always given Sangeeta a feeling of security, the feeling that all was right in the world. As demanding and exacting as her mother was, there was no denying the love she felt for her husband and the love he felt for her.

This was what she wanted. This was what she had not had with Param.

"Neepa. Don't give her a hard time." Her father chuckled. "I will take Sonny for a walk." He winked at his daughter.

"That's not necessary. It's so early—"

"Beti. I see how you look at each other. It is most definitely not too soon for this walk." He reached over and kissed her forehead.

Sangeeta opened her mouth to protest, but her father had already made his way to Sonny. He took Karina and handed her to Meeta Bhabi and spoke to Sonny. Sonny nodded and without a glance back at Sangeeta, joined her father as they made their way out the back door.

Oh boy.

June was most definitely hot and humid. The sun was just setting, but the stickiness in the air remained. Amol Uncle led them toward the backyard to pick up one of the many walking trails in this community. Sonny walked beside him and waited for him to speak. He assumed this was some kind of fatherly talk to warn him to be good to his daughter. Basically, the if-you-hurt-her-I-will-kill-you talk, which Sonny had thought he was going to get from Hiral, from the way he had been looking at him.

Sonny grinned to himself. He was getting this talk and he wasn't even in a real relationship.

Or so he had to keep reminding himself.

"You and Sangeeta have gotten together quite quickly." Amol Uncle stared straight ahead as he spoke, his voice calm, matter-of-fact.

"Yes." It was the truth.

"I can't help but wonder if there was more between you than anyone had thought last summer," Uncle commented, his voice even.

Silence seemed appropriate here, so Sonny said nothing. They continued to walk. "There is certainly something strong between you now."

Was there? They must be extremely good at acting.

"My daughter is brilliant, competent at many things, and very caring. But more than anything, my daughter is exacting. Much like her mother." Uncle's voice softened as he talked about his wife and daughter.

Sonny smiled and nodded. There had been no doubt as to that.

"It takes a unique man to be with such a woman."

Sonny's smile diminished some. Was Uncle about to tell him he did not have what it took to be with Sangeeta?

"I tell you this, not as a warning but as a fact." Uncle stopped walking and faced Sonny, his kind brown eyes squinting at him in the sun. "You will be the one who gets hurt in this, if you are not aware."

"You're concerned about my feelings? About my welfare?" Sonny was surprised.

Uncle looked at him as if this was obvious. "Of course. If things don't work out between you and San-

geeta, my daughter will be fine. She's strong and resil-
ient." He paused and frowned a bit. "She ran from her
wedding because it wasn't right for her. She ran in front
of hundreds of people—family, friends—because she
realized she did not want what was being offered. That
is strength." He sighed on a smile. "It would have been
preferable for my daughter to come to that realization
prior to that moment, but that is wishful thinking." He
nodded at Sonny. "Now, if it was Param or marriage she
ran from…" The older man shrugged. "I don't know if
even she knows just yet. Though you may want to find
that out before you get in too deep."

Sonny nodded. He did not have the answer to that
question. He did not need to know the answer. This was
fake. Though she had said that she ran from Param, not
from marriage itself.

Uncle smiled at him with maybe a bit of melancholy.
"Though it seems you may be in deeper than even you
thought."

Sonny had no idea what his face revealed, so he
said nothing.

They walked back, and Uncle changed the subject to
The Masala Hut and the various foods Sonny wanted
to introduce. Sonny tried to keep up, but his mind kept
wandering. Did Sangeeta leave Param, or did she leave
marriage?

They returned to the house and its very central family kitchen. Neepa Auntie was at the stove with Seema
Auntie. They seemed to be having a mild disagreement
about the way to cook something. Uncle walked past
his wife, brushing her shoulder gently with his hand as
he reached for a samosa.

If Sonny hadn't been watching so closely, he might have missed the small smile that fell over Neepa Auntie's face at the touch of her husband's hand. It warmed him to his core. Sangeeta had grown up with a similar example as he did. This was what he wanted. What did Sangeeta want?

And why did he care?

Chapter Twenty-Three

Sangeeta squirmed in the fitted dress she had just squeezed her body into. Reena had insisted she wear it to Asha's party, as apparently nothing Sangeeta owned was quite right. It was too hot for Spanx, so she had foregone it.

Asha Gupta was having a party. They were a month out from the wedding, and there was a ton of work to do, but Asha wanted to have a party, and she had insisted that Sangeeta and Sonny attend, and bring their friends.

"Stop squirming, you look amazing," Sonny said as the four of them rode the elevator up to Asha's penthouse flat. He ran his gaze over her, a small smirk on his lips. "This is a good look for you."

Sangeeta rolled her eyes at him. "It's just Tina and Reena right now. You can save the charm for the party." But she stopped squirming.

"So, you think I'm charming," he whispered in her ear, as he placed his hand at the small of her back and the elevator doors opened right into Asha's party.

If his comment and his look had not heated her, his hand right there did. His look was certainly not hurting him. Pink button-down with dark jeans, gray vest with the top button undone, the sleeves rolled up, revealing those fabulous forearms. She bit back her grin of pleasure from his compliment. "Ha."

"That's it? No 'you look nice too'?" He spoke softly so only she could hear as they exited the elevator into the party.

She drew her gaze up and down him, and cocked her head with a one-shouldered shrug, but said nothing. Truth was she couldn't say anything. She couldn't trust what would come out of her mouth.

Just then, Nila and Payal joined them. Nila was simply gorgeous in flowing summer dress., and the happy flush on her face as she held Payal's hand. "Hey! So glad you could all make it. Asha's in here."

The four of them followed the couple through dozens of people until they found Asha, who squealed with delight upon seeing them. She was gorgeous in a tight white dress, dark hair cascading down her back. "Hey! So happy you could make it." Rahul was next to her. Asha leaned into him and then looked back at them. "We both are." The way Asha looked at him left no question as to her feelings for him. It was wonderful to see someone so in love. Asha handed them champagne from a tray. "Have a drink—mingle!"

Sangeeta and Sonny circulated as a couple. Sangeeta saw Reena take Tina around and introduce her. People seemed to already know who they were. It was off-putting. Sonny took her hand, and she clung to it.

After a bit, Asha found them again, and introduced them to some of her friends. "You know, we don't know the story of how you met," Asha said. She took a seat on Rahul's lap, and her friends all sat around them. "Do tell."

Sonny looked at her. They were the only ones standing. She smiled and nodded. *Just tell the truth.*

"Well, I was at the beach last summer and I saw Sangeeta having a drink. Alone."

"Which is allowed," she interjected. She caught his eye with a smile, and she knew that he understood that playful was how they were going to get through this. People laughed.

He nodded acquiescence. "True. She was…" He locked his eyes with hers, and she was taken back to that moment. He lowered his voice. "…gorgeous. So, of course, I looked again." He turned back to the crowd. "She was sitting with her beach chair right at the edge of the water and as I passed her, I noticed that she was spooning the ice out of her drink and tossing it on the sand." He side-smiled at her, amusement in his eyes as he recalled the moment. "I said that she was wasting perfectly good ice."

Sangeeta jumped in, laughing. "My drink was cold. The ice had done its job." She shrugged.

Sonny had stopped midstep and turned to face her. She was under an umbrella, just her in her lounge chair with a book and a small cooler she was using as a table.

"You're firing the ice," he had said as he stepped closer.

"I don't like a watered-down drink." She had pursed her lips. *"Especially now."* Her mouth had turned down a bit, but then she returned to her drink.

"It was brilliant." Sonny chuckled. "I was instantly taken."

"But he kept walking," Sangeeta said, watching him. A gasp went through the crowd.

"Later that night I was at the bar—" Sonny started.

"Alone," added Sangeeta with a small smile.

"I had ordered a drink that came with ice," Sonny continued. The guests were enamored by him, their attention fixed as he took a few steps and moved his hands while telling the story. Even Sangeeta found herself unable to look away from him. "I was contemplating it when I heard the sexiest voice behind me say—"

"Give him a spoon," Sangeeta finished. Did he say her voice was sexy?

He smirked at Sangeeta, his gaze intense and playful, in a way that made her insides giddy. "The bartender gave me a spoon and gave her a drink. She sat down next to me." His voice softened. "We talked for hours."

"We walked on the beach when the bar closed." Sangeeta remembered how easy it had been to be in Sonny's presence.

"Then we stayed up all night talking in the lobby." Sonny fixed his gaze on her. She couldn't speak. The silence in the room was thick for a moment. They had stayed up all night, unaware of that fact until the sun had started to rise. Time had passed so quickly as they had talked and laughed all night. Sangeeta couldn't remember ever being at such ease with anyone before or since. She had told him as much. "The sunrise that morning was unlike any other I'd ever seen."

It was true.

Three days later, she'd left to go back to Param and her safe, organized life.

"That has to be the most adorable meet-cute ever!" Asha's eyes were filled with tears. "You two are so..." She raised a glass of champagne and looked around for everyone to follow suit. "To Sonny and Sangeeta and true love."

Everyone chorused her and clanked glasses and sipped their champagne.

"I do believe we need a kiss," Asha playfully suggested, a twinkle in her eye.

"Oh no. That's not—"

"Oh no, we don't have to—"

They both started protesting, putting distance between them. But Asha pulled them closer to each other. He smelled lightly of his cologne, and maybe some spice that was now part of his skin. Their shoulders were touching as they looked away from each other to continue protesting the kiss, and maybe find a way out. Asha stepped back and held up her phone.

"Aw, come on. One little kiss. For the followers."

Sangeeta turned toward him first. She could not afford to disappoint Asha. He turned toward her, a hard look in his eyes. He clearly did not want to do this. Well, neither did she. Not really.

She looked him in the eye and bounced her head back and forth. *Give them what they want. How hard could it be?*

He widened his eyes. *Hell no. I draw the line here. Enough is enough.*

She narrowed her eyes, a small smirk on her mouth. *Are you afraid?*

He raised an eyebrow. *I am not afraid to kiss you.*

She shrugged one shoulder. *So give Asha what she wants.*

He rolled his eyes and leaned down and pecked her on the lips. They were met with a round of boos.

He sighed as he looked at her, and in that split second, she saw a glint in his eye, and then they softened, and everything and everyone around them disappeared.

He cupped her cheek with one hand, his calluses rough against her skin, and slowly lowered his head until his lips just barely touched hers, sipping at her. She automatically lifted her face to his, pressing her lips against his more firmly, suddenly hungry for his kiss. She was in the rain with him and there was no one else and everything she had desired in that moment was coming to her. In this moment when neither of them seemed capable of holding back.

He pulled her closer, his hand tightening on her cheek. She opened her mouth to him and he responded to her, grunting as if there was a war within him. His kiss had started out careful, guarded, but now he let go, kissing her as if she were all he'd ever wanted. And she responded in kind. Kissing Param had never felt like this. Kissing any other man had never felt like this.

So all-consuming, so good. So right.

Then all at once, the sound of cheering reached her. She didn't care. She leaned in to keep kissing this man. To keep kissing Sonny. But he froze and pulled back.

Before he turned away, she caught his look of surprise and regret.

Crap. What was showing on her face?

She brought her hand to her lips and faced Asha, who was leading the cheering. She caught Reena and Tina staring at them from across the room, their mouths agape.

What had just happened?

Chapter Twenty-Four

He had not just kissed Sangeeta for real. That would be crazy. But he had.

And it was amazing.

Because she'd kissed him back.

Now, everyone was watching them.

But all he could see was her. Her lips were wet from his kiss, and she was flushed. He could still taste her. Flashes were going off.

Her eyes started to show panic. Her body was going rigid. They needed to leave.

"We should go," he whispered.

She nodded at him.

He wrapped his arm around her and drew her to his body, as if shielding her from the crowd. To the onlookers, he said, "We need to call it a night."

This news resulted in an abundance of groans. He

grinned at them. "My girl has a wedding to plan." He put himself between her and them. Her heart pounded fast and hard against him. They needed to leave now. "Not to mention, that was some hot kiss, am I right?" He winked at the guests, and that did it. They broke into laughter and acquiesced to let lovers go home and do what lovers did.

Though none of that would be happening. No matter how right it felt to call her his girl. He held her close and guided her toward the cove where the elevator was.

Sangeeta was stiff but followed his lead. She seemed as eager to leave the party as he was. In fact, if he looked close enough, she had a slightly dazed and flushed look about her. He had put that flush in her cheeks.

Maybe everything was not as fake as they were making it out to be. Maybe this could be real. He allowed himself that spark of hope.

They waited in silence for the elevator to make it to the penthouse. The sounds of the party felt as if they came from far away, like they were in a bubble.

Sangeeta looked straight ahead at the mirrored elevator doors. "It wasn't real." She spoke softly. Interesting how she could crumble his hope without even moving her lips.

His heart fell into his stomach. He didn't know what he had expected her to say, but it wasn't that. He looked at her in the mirror and fixed his expression. "Of course it wasn't."

"I mean, you're a…good kisser and everything, but just a reminder to you that we are faking this."

He straightened his shoulders and pulled down at his

vest before folding his hands in front of him and steeling his expression. "Yep. Nothing between us is real."

"There is nothing between us." She looked at him in the mirror, her mouth set, eyes pleading. He'd never seen that look before. She did not *want* there to be anything between them. "We are simply faking."

Though did the distinction even matter?

He clenched his teeth to further steel his expression and nodded. He wasn't sure what he would say if he spoke. *Don't be ridiculous. I know you felt something in that kiss. It was no ordinary kiss.* But to what end? She clearly did not want anything with him outside this fake relationship.

How long was the elevator going to take?

"You're faking?" A deep voice came around the corner of the small cove.

Panic flooded his body as he saw in the mirrored elevator doors that it was Rahul who spoke.

Sonny and Sangeeta glanced at each other in the mirror, his panic reflected in her eyes. Before they could confirm or deny, Rahul grinned and spoke again.

"Makes sense. You both need this wedding. Asha is taken with your 'romance.'" He nodded, a grimace across his face. "No point in denying it to me." He paused. "I'll keep your secret. It makes no difference to me if your relationship is real or not. The wedding is all Asha's show. I just need to marry her." He glared at them in the mirror. "Just keep Asha happy, and I'll keep your secret."

The elevator doors opened. Sonny followed Sangeeta in. They turned and faced Rahul as the elevator doors shut.

* * *

"Oh my god. He knows, he knows, he knows, he knows." Sangeeta paced the small elevator. She was going to lose this wedding, and then her job. She would have no way of paying her parents back, she'd have no livelihood. She might even have to go back to living with her parents in India. Her world was a complete jumble again, but the thing that was foremost in her mind was that kiss.

She tried to push aside how his mouth had felt on hers, how in that moment she hadn't been able to get enough. She meant what she had said. There was nothing between them. She didn't want there to be. It was too complicated. Skin-melting kiss or not.

"He's not going to say anything." Sonny was standing to the side of the elevator, still looking drop-dead gorgeous in his light gray vest and pants. He was currently unbuttoning the vest. Damn.

Sangeeta stopped. "That's weird, right?"

Sonny nodded agreement, not looking at her.

"How do we know for sure he's not going to say something?" Sangeeta started pacing again.

"We don't."

"We didn't confirm or deny, so even if he said something, we could easily deny—"

"He probably recorded us." Sonny seemed sure of himself.

Made sense. "So what do we do?"

He shrugged. "We wait and see. If he tells, we'll know by morning."

The Uber was waiting for them, courtesy of Reena and Lulu's. Sonny opened the door and she scooted over, giving him room. "Wait and see? That's your plan?" Sangeeta nearly squealed. That wasn't a plan, that was an un-plan. "No. We need to head this off." She took her phone out. "Let me text Asha. I'll explain—"

"No." Sonny took her hands in both of his and pulled them to him, forcing her to look at him. There was no hesitation in him. She was once again in his bubble of spice, and the last hints of musk from whatever cologne he had splashed on earlier. His hands were slightly coarse, but warm, his grip firm. "Letting things play out is a plan. It's just a plan that involves letting go of some control."

"I can't."

"You have to. Texting Asha if Rahul has not said anything will only alert Asha to the possibility of a problem, where right now, Asha thinks we're really together. Especially after…" He leaned back and dropped her hands. "Just don't text her." He settled into his side of the seat and turned to face out the window.

As much as she hated to admit it, he was right.

"Promise me you won't text her." He spoke to the window.

"Okay," Sangeeta agreed.

The Uber pulled up in front of The Masala Hut and they both got out of the car. She led the way to the back and opened the lock with the key Sonny had made her. She felt him behind her, with an awareness she hadn't experienced before. She opened the door to the apartment and tried to push aside all Sonny-kiss-related thoughts. No small feat, since they were now in his space. All the smells and sounds were of him.

They were alone.

She needed this night to end. Sonny took off his shoes, tossed off his vest and untucked his shirt before heading for the small kitchen. He started pulling out vegetables and bread. He pulled out two glasses and poured a finger of bourbon into each. She stepped out of the dreaded heels, suddenly ravenous.

"We left without eating." He sipped his bourbon as he prepared chutney sandwiches for them.

She sat in a barstool by the raised kitchen bar. There was nothing to say. They had needed to leave after that phenomenal kiss. He met her eyes but said nothing. The only sounds were of Sonny making them sandwiches.

"Are we going to talk about it?" he asked finally, still seemingly engrossed in his work.

"We already did," Sangeeta replied, not making eye contact.

"Seriously? You felt nothing?" His voice was low and gravelly. Honestly, did he do that on purpose because she felt the vibration of his voice all through her.

"I felt nothing. There was nothing to feel. It's all an act, right?" Stay the course. She had no idea what her feelings were at this time. Only that he was standing mere feet from her, feeding her, asking her to talk about her feelings and all she wanted to do was just kiss him again.

He cut the sandwiches in half into triangles, which was, of course, the only way to cut a sandwich.

He finished his bourbon as he placed a plate in front of her. "It started out as act, Sangeeta." His voice was soft and intimate with an edge of irritation. "But that kiss, that was not an act. Not for me." He placed his naked forearms on the granite and leaned toward her, gripping her gaze with his. "Not for you."

She needed to pry her gaze away from him, but it was impossible. He was hypnotizing. His lips moved as he spoke, taunting her. No. She could not possibly have feelings for him. Not so soon after breaking up with Param. This was lust. And it would pass.

"Hormones." She pulled her plate to her.

"We're not teenagers." Sonny chuckled.

Even his damn chuckle was sexy. She stood up straighter away from the granite counter, trying to put a few extra inches between them. "That kiss was an act. For both of us. It has to be."

"Why? Why does it have to be?" His voice was still low, but he seemed somehow closer to her, so she could feel the air vibrate again when he spoke.

"Because I was about to get married four weeks ago." She forced herself to look up at him. He was an open book. Vulnerability in his eyes softened her resolve. *Because she was afraid of hurting him.*

"We met months ago." He threw those words at her with a frustration she hadn't seen before.

"We hung out for three days nine months ago. It means nothing." Stay the course. She couldn't afford to cave in to that look in his eyes, or the fact that his frustration was simply a mirror to how much he wanted her.

"Prove it."

"What do you mean 'prove it'? I don't have to prove anything to you." That was it. Indignation would help her stay strong.

"So, kiss me again." His voice was even and rational now, as if challenging someone to kiss him was a reasonable request.

"Wh-why?" The thought of kissing him again, of melting away into him once again—no—she shook her head and stood up straight again, desperate to build a wall between her and everything about him. "There's no need—"

Sonny slowly walked around to her side of the granite bar and stood next to her. Not quite in her space, not quite touching her, but close enough. "If you can kiss me again and swear that you feel nothing, I'll drop it." He stepped into her space. "But I felt something, and I know you did too."

She looked up at him and swallowed. He was so close, and he smelled so good. She closed her eyes and imagined giving in to what her heart and body wanted. Her heart and body, but not her mind. Her mind sent up a klaxon. Danger! Danger! Danger! You'll hurt him like you hurt Param. He's only in this to help his sister. But it never *felt* like this with Param, a smaller voice protested.

"How could I possibly have feelings—real feelings—for you when four weeks ago I was getting ready to marry Param?" She shook her head. "It doesn't make sense."

His top button was undone, and a slight scruff had started to form on his fabulous jaw. Those wonderful warm brown eyes watched her, waiting for her to give in. She could have sworn that he was holding his breath. "It does not have to make sense, Sangeeta."

"I felt nothing." Her voice trembled, belying her words. "I kissed you because the moment required it—

because it was part of the plan. Kissing you right now would serve no purpose. Kissing you here and now is not part of the plan."

He raised an eyebrow at her and bit his bottom lip. "That's the beauty of it."

She wanted to be the one biting that lip. His breath mingled with hers, he had moved that close. She reached out and touched his chest, grazing it, really, hardly a touch. His eyelids fluttered a second, and he swallowed hard as if her touch was tantalizing. He focused on her again.

She should step back and eat her sandwich. She should run as fast as she could from this man. This man who had her completely captivated, once again. This man who was completely under her power as he waited for her to kiss him. She pressed her hand against the muscles in his chest and was rewarded with the slightest gasp. She leaned in, their lips almost touching. She couldn't remember ever wanting anything this deeply. She wanted his lips on hers again, because having them there earlier had felt natural, right, good. Her mind shut down and her lips touched his. That was all it took. Sonny opened his mouth and pressed against her and she was surprised sparks didn't fly from her lips to his.

If that kiss at the party was for everyone, this kiss was just for them. He tasted like the bourbon he'd been drinking, sweet and smoky. She stood on tiptoe so she could reach him better. He lifted her onto the stool, his mouth never leaving hers, his hands—*his amazing hands*—never leaving her body. He deepened their kiss, covering her almost entirely with his body. She pressed against him, moving on instinct and need. Her clothes became impediments to feeling those hands on her. She wanted to undo her dress zipper, but that would mean taking her hands off his muscles, off his body, and right now that was unthinkable.

As if he could read her mind, Sonny reached for the dress zipper, his whisper low and gruff. "Invite me to bed, Sangeeta." His fingers hovered over the zipper as he waited for her answer.

"You'll have to unzip this dress first."

No sooner had she finished speaking than the zipper was down, the dress falling from her shoulders. "As you wish." He kissed her exposed shoulders and neck, his mouth cool on her hot skin.

She reached her arms around his neck and whispered, "Take me to bed, Sonny."

He picked her up in his arms, as gently as he had that day she cut herself, and carried her to his bed.

Months of yearning poured out of him, and he didn't care. He didn't care that she would at once know his feelings for her. This was right. She was the one. He'd been in love with her all this time, denying it because he never thought she could feel the same way. But maybe she did.

He surrendered to her everything he had, relishing every inch of her, over and over, before they finally fell asleep together, their legs entwined, spent and exhausted.

His contentment lasted until first light. Which was when Sangeeta sat bolt upright in bed.

"Oh my god! What did we do? What did we do?"

Sonny rolled over lazily. "Well, we started with just

kissing, but then you asked me to take your dress off so we—"

She smacked him.

"Ow."

"What. Did. We. Do?"

"We…um…well…" He put his arm around her and pulled her toward him. He was languid and content. "It's easier if I show you." He kissed the soft skin of her neck, felt her pulse quicken. Her breath caught, making his heart race, so he continued working his way south.

He hadn't gotten nearly as far as he would have liked when she sat up again. "We can't keep doing this."

"Sure we can." He smirked at her.

"No. Sonny." She put her hands on his face and turned him to look at her. Her eyes were sad, and her mouth had that set look she got when she was afraid or planning.

Huh.

"We can't. We never should have—we need to forget." She hopped out of bed, dragging the sheets with her to cover her body. "That's what we'll do." She was talking fast and nodding quickly as she kept the sheets covering what Sonny had known and had confirmed was a beautifully curvaceous and luscious body. It was hard to concentrate on what she was saying.

"Okay?" She was looking at him, waiting for an answer.

"Okay what?"

"Okay we'll pretend this never happened. It'll be just like normal. We're faking a relationship to save our jobs. My job and your sister's hotel."

"You want to pretend we didn't just have sex so we

can pretend we're in a relationship?" Sonny sat up and narrowed his eyes at her.

"Yes. It's a perfectly good plan."

"Or we can just go with this." He grinned. "We can acknowledge that we had great sex and have a real relationship."

He knew the minute the words came out of his mouth that he had said the wrong thing. Her face paled, her eyes grew wide and she started shaking her head back and forth.

"No. No. No. That will never work." She shook her head with vehemence, a frown on her face.

He held out his hands as if he had spooked her. "Sangeeta. It's okay. Let's slow down. Back it up a bit."

She stopped shaking her head. But she stood there looking at him, frozen to her spot. "Can we agree that we had fun last night?" he asked slowly.

She nodded her head slowly. He grinned and moved to edge of the bed and kneeled up to her. He tugged gently at the sheet and she stepped closer to him.

"It was pretty amazing," he said softly.

She rewarded him with her smile. "It really was." She sighed.

He leaned in to kiss her.

"But it shouldn't have happened," she blurted out.

He stopped and looked at her. "What do you mean?"

"I mean, I had...fun. But it should not have happened. It won't happen again." She tugged at the sheet, pulled away from him and ran into the bathroom.

Chapter Twenty-Five

Oh crap. What had she done? And why did she want to get back into that bed and do it again?

She could *not* get involved with Sonny Pandya.

Not for real. He said *real relationship*.

She couldn't do that. She would do nothing but hurt him. She was ready to marry Param four weeks ago. Any feelings she had right now were rebound feelings, weren't they? Though she had never had feelings like this for anyone. Not only did she want to jump right back into bed with Sonny, but she wanted to be held by him, she wanted to work with him and fight with him and laugh with him, all at the same time.

It was too much. Too soon. She had been with Param for close to two years, thinking that she loved him, only to leave him at the mandap. She didn't have the foggiest idea what a *real* relationship entailed. What was the guarantee she wouldn't hurt Sonny, too?

All the more reason to keep her distance. She closed her eyes and Param's pained face came to her. She had caused that pain because she hadn't been honest with herself. Because she'd had to stick to her plan. Because her feeling of security had been more important than opening herself up to him, to sharing her true self—with Param. She deserved to feel guilty for hurting him when it could have been avoided. She would not do that again. Not to anyone.

Especially Sonny Pandya.

She showered and changed and gathered herself. When she came out of the bathroom, she smelled coffee brewing, but Sonny was back in bed.

"What's going on, Sangeeta?"

She shrugged, her resolve stronger now. "Nothing. We slept together. It doesn't have to mean anything. People sleep together all the time."

"I know that people sleep together all the time." He focused that soft brown gaze solidly on her, as if he wanted to be sure she heard him. "I'm telling you that I have feelings for you. That this wasn't just 'people sleeping together.' Not for me."

"You're a hopeless romantic, then." She met his eyes and caught the pain that flashed in them before he could hide it from her.

"You're saying that you have no feelings for me. That you felt nothing. This was casual."

"That is precisely what I am saying." She avoided his eyes.

"You're lying to yourself." Sonny clenched his jaw

and shook his head. His whole body hardened, in contrast to his voice. "We could be good together, Sangeeta."

"We won't be anything together." She stayed firm. She knew she was hurting him, but better to nip this in the bud now.

Sonny watched her for a minute. Then he hopped out of bed, no longer naked. "Okay."

"Okay?"

"Yes. Okay."

Sangeeta was confused. He had just been talking about a real relationship, and now he was okay with her rejection.

He was making the bed and looked at her. "Don't you have to get to work?" He gathered up his clothes and went to the bathroom. "I need to get downstairs. Dharm is going to give me crap for being late. See you later."

Sangeeta stared at the bathroom door, not sure what was going on. She poured herself a cup of coffee from the pot Sonny had started and yawned. She needed to focus. The shower turned on. And not on the fact that Sonny was currently naked in the bathroom. She poured her coffee into a to-go cup, grabbed her bag and left. She would have to forgo her usual chai today. She tapped her phone for the Uber, and the car was waiting for her by the time she got outside. She needed to stop by The Posh and check on a few things. First, she had a meeting with Asha at noon.

The Uber dropped her off at a coffee shop across from the The Posh. She pulled out her computer and tried to concentrate on flowers and food. She worked until Asha showed up.

"Oh, hey honey!" Asha teased. "I saw you and Sonny

cut out early last night." She side-eyed her meaning-fully. "I hope you had a fabulous evening."

Sangeeta plastered a smile to her face. "It was amazing." She wasn't lying.

"That's it?" Asha raised an eyebrow. "That's all we get?"

"Asha." Sangeeta pursed her lips and shook her head. "Come on."

Asha raised her hands in surrender. "Fine, don't kiss and tell. I'm just happy that someone got some action last night. Since I most certainly did not."

Panic flooded Sangeeta. "What do you mean?"

"Rahul had a business call. He was out half the night." Asha shrugged. "It happens. Don't let that happen to you and Sonny. Work is important, but make time for each other."

Sangeeta nodded. "Have you talked to him about it?"

"Of course, but you love who you love, you know? Like you and Sonny. Sure, you were about to marry what's-his-name a few weeks ago, but it's so clear that you and Sonny are meant for each other."

"Is it?" Sangeeta's stomach dropped.

"Well, I mean, yeah. If you're looking. I know some people would be like, 'Oh no, it's too soon after Param. Sonny is the rebound guy.'" Asha shook her head. "But he's so not. It's clear you two have a connection. A true bond." Asha paused. "I've only known you a short time, but you don't always see how you two look at each other, the way you two are so in sync with one another, even when you disagree." Her voice had softened, and her eyes were misty. "You certainly came together in a convoluted way, but that's just life making it interesting. It's a rare thing, Sangeeta. Cherish it."

Sangeeta stared at her. "I—I don't—"

"There's nothing to say. Just remember that, one girlfriend to another." Asha squeezed her hand.

"I will." Sangeeta nodded. Maybe she had been too rash this morning. Maybe running from Param was just her path. To teach her what she needed to know. She shook her head. She still had work to do. "Shall we get started?"

"Sure."

Sangeeta and Asha went over plans for the wedding and its preliminary events. "Your guests will fill almost every room at Lulu's, so you'll have that intimate feeling, like the space is only for you and Rahul."

Asha beamed. "I love it."

The meeting ran longer than she had expected. It was nearly 4:00 p.m. when Sangeeta stood. "I need to go across the street and settle a few things—nothing for you to be concerned with, I promise. So go do more fun wedding stuff. I'll text you later."

Asha beamed. "What would I do without a friend like you?" Asha hugged her and left.

Huh. Who would have thought she would start to like Asha Gupta? Sangeeta marched across the street prepared to do some battle with the event coordinator in getting some money back for Asha.

It wasn't as hard as she'd expected. After a bit of cajoling, partnered with logic and the law, the event coordinator for The Posh gave up a sum that they agreed was fair. Sangeeta suspected the woman simply wanted to be done with the whole affair.

Sangeeta headed down the elevator feeling lighter and pretty good about herself, at least as a professional. Thoughts of Sonny kept invading her thoughts, but she wasn't necessarily upset by that. She closed her eyes and let go for a moment.

The doors of the elevator opened and she stepped out. The elevator doors across from her opened at the same time.

Which was when she saw him.

Rahul.

He was still in the elevator, unaware that the doors had opened. But then, how could he be aware of elevator doors, when he had his tongue down some woman's throat and his hands squeezing her ass.

"Rahul?" Sangeeta cried out before she could stop herself.

He started at the sound of his name, and paled when he saw her.

"Rahul?" She glanced at the woman. "What is going on here?"

Rahul stepped off the elevator just as the doors closed, leaving the woman on the cart. "What are you doing here?"

"My job!"

"Is it now your job to spy on me?"

"I'm not spying on you. I came to get money—never mind. What the hell are you doing with your tongue down another woman's throat?"

"That's not what happened."

"I saw it with my own eyes." Sangeeta burned with the audacity of this man. *She just saw him.*

"That's not proof."

"I do not lie." Sangeeta narrowed her eyes at him.

"Don't you, though?" Rahul smirked at her.

Sangeeta faltered and he had her.

"If you breathe a word of this to Asha, I'll tell her about your little scheme. And unlike you, I have proof." He tapped his phone and turned it toward Sangeeta.

She found herself watching a video of herself and Sonny staring at each other in the mirrored elevator doors, clearly stating that they were faking their relationship for Asha. If she saw this, all would be over. Everything would be lost.

Sangeeta glared at Rahul. "You're cheating on her. She loves you completely, and you're sleeping around."

"No different than what you're doing. You need her notoriety. And so do I. So don't get high and mighty on me. You keep your mouth shut, no one has a problem," Rahul spit at her.

Sangeeta turned on her heel and marched away. She was so angry she walked the fifteen blocks back to The Masala Hut in the rain.

She needed to talk to Sonny.

Sonny spent the day practicing the items for the wedding menu, as well as dealing with the rainy day crowd. Nothing like rain to have people running for comfort food.

Sangeeta had been gone when he got out of the bathroom. She could run, but how long could she hide from her feelings? He couldn't force her to acknowledge her feelings any more than he could deny his.

He was falling for Sangeeta.

No. That wasn't true.

He had already fallen for her. He was in love with her. If he was honest, he had been since they met on the beach. He tried to stop it, but he couldn't. He never should have let her go all those months ago, but he certainly would not be backing off without a fight now. He had until this wedding was over.

He was getting ready for the afternoon rush when Sangeeta barged into the kitchen. "Sonny. We need to talk."

"I'm prepping for the afternoon chai crowd," he said without turning around.

"Sonny. Seriously. We have a problem."

The edge of desperation in her voice made him turn to her. She was wet and disheveled, her eyes darting all around. "Did you just get caught in the rain?"

"I walked here from The Posh." She glanced around the kitchen at their audience. "Office." She marched back to his office.

Sonny found a couple of towels and a blanket in his office closet. He wrapped her in one towel to keep her from shivering while he dried her with the other. She was shivering, her jaw was set, and there was panic in her eyes. She probably barely registered that he was touching her. When he was through, he wrapped her in the blanket and shut the door.

"Get the blinds too."

He did as she asked and then sat down next to her on the sofa. If not for the panicked look on her face, he might have thrilled at having this level of privacy with her.

"Rahul is cheating on Asha." The words tumbled out of her as if they had been poisoning her.

"What?"

"I saw him—them. Making out in an elevator when I went to The Posh. Which is quite smart of him, because Asha can't go to The Posh anymore, so why would he think he would get caught. But he did. I caught him." Sangeeta paced and talked, wrapped in the blanket, the words quickly leaving her.

Sonny watched her, and then waited for her to stop for breath before he spoke. "Start over and go slow."

"I saw Rahul kissing a woman who wasn't Asha in an elevator in The Posh. I confronted him and he threatened to tell Asha about our faking if I told her about him." She stopped to breathe. "You were right. He has video of our conversation."

Sonny stared at her, fuming. He had come to like Asha this past month or so. But even if he hadn't, cheating was low. Then they both spoke at the same time. "We have to tell her."

They smiled at each other. "We'll lose everything," Sangeeta said. "Reena will lose the hotel—your dad will sell to that company. She'll be—"

"Pissed and heartbroken," Sonny said. "You'll lose your job. Clients will be hard to come by. This whole thing will be public."

Sangeeta nodded. "You should have seen him. He wasn't even apologetic. He doesn't even care about Asha." She looked at Sonny, the horror of it in her eyes. "He was right about one thing—we're using Asha too." She pressed her lips together. "We're really no better than he is."

It was the truth. "We need proof before we go to her."

"I don't know how we're supposed to get that." Sangeeta shook her head. "The wedding is weeks away. And he knows I'm onto him."

Sonny stared off into space, then turned to her. "I have an idea."

Chapter Twenty-Six

"Reena." Sangeeta opened the door, as if she really lived in this apartment. She looked behind Reena as if she could have been followed. "Come in. Did you get it?" Her voice was hushed.

"Yes. What's going on?" Reena entered the apartment, a frown on her face.

Sonny put his hand out, and she handed him the thumb drive.

"One of you needs to say something. I'm getting a very creepy vibe here." Reena looked from Sangeeta to Sonny and back again.

Sonny plugged the USB into his computer. "Well, your vibe is correct. We'll show you in a minute."

Sangeeta's heart lifted. He believed her 100 percent. He had her back. Sonny looked at her. "What time?"

"About 4:30 p.m. yesterday." Sangeeta walked over

to the computer to see. Reena stood on the other side of Sonny.

Sangeeta and Sonny had stayed up late the night before, going over the situation. They had ordered takeout and mulled things over. No matter how they looked at it, no matter how they tried to salvage everything, the reality was that once Asha found out that Rahul was cheating on her, she would cancel her wedding. And honestly, neither of them could blame her.

Except everyone would lose something in the end, since Rahul would most definitely out their fake relationship in retaliation. Either way, there would be no wedding, Sangeeta stood to lose whatever goodwill she might have garnered, and Sonny would lose the opportunity to show his parents what he really could do.

And Reena would lose the hotel.

"What if we didn't tell her?" Sangeeta had asked.

Sonny had given her a withering look. "We aren't those people, Sangeeta."

She had tried to ignore how comforting it felt to have Sonny refer to them as a "we." But it felt good to be a "we" with Sonny.

She just didn't know what she wanted right now.

"I know. Of course we have to tell her." Sangeeta was curled up on the sofa, her back leaning against Sonny's chest, as they each nursed a glass of wine. His heart beating gently into her back.

"There's no other choice." He breathed the words into her ear, and she sank into him. "You stand to lose your reputation—people may not want to hire you."

"I lost all that when I ran from my wedding. This

was a spark of hope." She shrugged. "What about you? And Reena? The hotel is all she thinks about."

"Reena is quite tough. As her older brother who had to get her out of more than one situation growing up, I can tell you, she will survive." He raised his glass to her. "And so will I."

Sangeeta turned so she was facing him. "Me too." Silence had floated between them, comfortable and soft. "I guess the first thing I'll need is a place to stay."

"You can stay here as long as you want."

"I can't."

"No, really. Sangeeta." His voice had softened. "I wouldn't mind one bit. Just because you stay here, doesn't mean we have to share a bed." He had run his fingers lightly over her arm. "It doesn't mean we can't share a bed either." The way he had looked at her had melted, electrified and scared her all at once. It would be so easy to give in to him. To bask in his attention. To live here with him like a real couple.

But she'd always done easy. Param was easy. Planning every minute was easy, because it took out the risk. Maybe it was time to look inside herself, and see what else was there.

"You know I can't," she had whispered, unable to look at him.

"You say that, but what I hear is that you won't. You want to, but you won't." The way he had rested those deep brown eyes on her, she had been tempted to give in to her feelings.

"You could get hurt," she had said, tears burning at her eyes.

"That's my risk to take," he had said, leaning over

and kissing her hand, wrist, arm, melting every body part he touched, and some that melted in anticipation of his touch.

"Sonny."

"Mmm." He kissed her shoulder, neck, jaw.

"Sonny, please."

"Whatever you want, babe. Just say it." He continued kissing her.

She pulled away from him, taking his face in her hands. "Sonny. Stop." Tears had filled her eyes, blurring her vision, but it didn't stop her from seeing the surprise and hurt in his eyes. "I'm going to bed. Alone."

"We just need the camera footage from Reena. Then we'll go to Asha tomorrow," Sangeeta had said, ignoring what his eyes were saying.

She had stood and gone to the bedroom, shut the door and climbed into the bed. The bed that smelled like Sonny no matter how many times she washed the sheets.

She heard Sonny washing the wineglasses then getting the sofa ready for bed. She had lain in bed willing sleep to come, trying not to think about Sonny.

Sonny forwarded to the time Sangeeta had said and sure enough, there was Rahul with his hands all over a woman. A woman who, as Sangeeta had said, was not Asha.

"What a complete asshole," Sonny grumbled.

Reena watched them, then stepped back from the video. "This is what you wanted me to see? This is what I cashed in two favors for?"

"Well, we needed proof before we go to Asha," Sonny said.

Reena shook her head. "Go to Asha? Asha Gupta is our client, not our friend. This is not our business." She pulled the thumb drive from the computer.

"This is absolutely our business. He's cheating on her," said Sangeeta.

Reena stared them down. "If you tell her, Rahul will out your relationship as fake." She turned her hazel eyes on Sangeeta. "No one will want you to plan their wedding. You'd be deemed a liar." She turned to Sonny. "All that new business you're both enjoying will be gone. Not to mention that she would most likely cancel the wedding altogether." Reena grew pale, her eyes frantically dancing between the two of them. Sangeeta had never seen her like this. "The hotel will be lost. That bank will be ready to swoop in and take the hotel, so Papa will sell to that third party, whatever they're asking. We would lose the hotel." She shook her head. "No. We keep our mouths shut. Or we are all screwed."

Sangeeta shook her head. "No. Asha needs to know."

Reena looked at her brother. "Sonny. You can't let this happen. You promised to help me fix this."

"Fix this? Reena. Rahul is using Asha."

"So are we! I need—we need this, Sonny. There will be nothing left for me."

"Papa is not going to let you—"

"That's not the point. This hotel is our legacy. Papa was going to sell. I *begged* him for this chance. I promised that I would save the hotel. If we lose this wedding, I'll be a *failure*." Reena's voice cracked on the last word as if she'd never even said it before.

"No, you won't," Sangeeta spoke gently. "Just because

things aren't going as planned, doesn't mean that you're a failure. Sometimes, things don't go as planned."

Sonny glanced from his sister to Sangeeta and back. "Reena. You have lost your perspective here. Asha deserves to know the truth."

"Sonny, you promised you would always be there—I can't have this conversation with you right now." Reena was frantic, beside herself. She stormed out of the apartment.

"What just happened?" Sangeeta asked him.

Sonny shook his head. "I don't know. I'll talk to her in the morning. I haven't seen her like this often, but when I have, it hasn't been good." He looked around. "She took the thumb drive."

"I'll set up a meeting with Asha for tomorrow. If she needs to cancel the wedding, she may get some money back from some of the vendors." Sangeeta started calculating in her head. "Anyway. I'm going to bed."

Sonny stared at the door his sister had left from. "Yeah. Me too."

Chapter Twenty-Seven

"Asha should be here soon." Sangeeta glanced up from her phone. They were meeting her in the restaurant after hours so they could have some privacy. She paced while Sonny watched her. She wore a small cross-body to hold her phone that banged against her hip as she paced.

She stopped and they looked at each other. "We're doing the right thing."

"We are," Sonny agreed.

"I mean you'll get your apartment back. I'll be out of your hair."

"Right." Sonny nodded. "Unless you—"

"Reena will get over it, right?" Sangeeta cut him off. She couldn't have that conversation again. "She's your sister, after all."

At this Sonny's eyes went hard and he gave a one-shouldered shrug. "Reena is all about business, not feelings."

"Did you talk to her this morning?"

"I did. Got the thumb drive back too."

"And?"

Sonny's eyes hardened and he looked away as if unable to maintain eye contact with her. Before Sangeeta could press him further, the door opened and Asha entered with her brother and sister behind her. She looked fabulous as always, even in simple capri jeans and a sleeveless top.

"Hi." Sangeeta fidgeted, her voice a bit higher than normal. "Thanks for coming on such late notice."

"Yes. No problem." Asha narrowed her eyes at her. "Is everything okay? You sound funny. I texted Rahul, but I haven't heard from him."

"Oh. You told Rahul?" Sangeeta tried to maintain a straight face.

"Well, yes, he is my fiancé." Asha studied her harder. Sangeeta started to sweat.

It wasn't that she didn't like confrontation. She was fine with professional confrontation. She had plenty of it dealing with brides, their mothers, their maids of honor and any other person who had an opinion about a wedding. This felt more…personal. And personal confrontation was not her strong suit. Emotions were usually involved, and she got flustered. Which was another reason to have a plan. She could always fall back on the details of a plan if things got too…heavy. But there was no getting out of this. This conversation must be had, no matter how hard, no matter what she lost.

"I assume this has to do with the wedding?" Asha was still talking.

Sangeeta looked at Sonny and nodded. He placed the thumb drive in the computer and started typing.

"Well, sort of." Sangeeta moved toward Asha. "I'm sorry, Asha." She inhaled deeply. *Just say the words.* "I caught Rahul making out with another woman in the elevator of The Posh."

Nila groaned and Akash swore under his breath. Both siblings moved toward their sister. "I never trusted him—" Akash started, fisting his hands by his side.

Asha stared at Sangeeta, not moving, not even blinking.

"You are mistaken," Asha finally said, her lips pressed together. "You think you saw something—there's an explanation. Rahul loves me. He will explain."

"I am not mistaken, Asha." Sangeeta softened her voice. "I—" Sangeeta hesitated. "*We* have proof."

"She doesn't have to see it," said Sonny quietly from behind her.

"That's true, Asha. You really don't have to, but I do have proof."

"Asha. Sangeeta and I have no reason to lie to you. You must believe that," Sonny spoke. Sangeeta picked up a tinge of anxiety in his normally steady voice. Hmm. He probably didn't like having this conversation any more than she did.

"Show it to her," Nila spoke up quite firmly. "She needs to see." She nodded at her brother. He agreed.

"Sonny?" Sangeeta asked, but Sonny made eye contact with her and gave a slight shake to his head.

What? Sangeeta leaned over and looked. Sonny

had it at the time she had mentioned. But the elevator showed a family simply going up the elevator. The video was gone. "What did you do?" she whispered, as Rahul came running in.

"What's going on?" He glanced at his watch, the picture of innocence. Sangeeta fought the urge to punch him. "I got here as fast as I could."

"What's going on is that Sangeeta and Sonny say they caught you with another woman," Akash said.

Rahul furrowed his brow and shook his head, the picture of innocence. "What? That's ridiculous. Why would I do that?"

"I don't know. Why don't you tell us?" Sangeeta asked, her voice loud and clear and accusatory.

He ignored Sangeeta. "My love. I would never do such a thing. I have no desire for anyone else but you."

Asha smiled at him, her face full of love. It was the saddest beautiful thing Sangeeta had ever seen. Rahul did not deserve that kind of love. And Asha deserved better. Everyone did. She shot a look at Sonny. *Get the video!*

He pressed his lips together and gave a slight shake of his head. There was no video.

Nila stepped up and spoke gently to her sister. "Sangeeta has proof. Let's see." Nila made eye contact with Sangeeta, pleading with her in that moment to convince her sister of the truth.

Sangeeta pressed her lips together, giving Sonny the side-eye. She had no idea what had happened to that video. All she knew was that it was there last night and now it wasn't. Sonny had gone to speak with Reena this morning, and now the video was gone. "It seems—"

she wiped sweat from her upper lip "—that the video is not there anymore." She glared at Sonny, who had the audacity to look confused.

"Why are you lying to me like this, Sangeeta? I thought you were my friend." Asha turned her hostility on her.

"I am your friend. That's why I need you to believe me. I can get proof—"

"I know why she's lying to you about us. It's to discredit me. Because they are the ones cheating you, Asha," Rahul spoke, pulling out his phone. "Sangeeta and Sonny aren't really a couple. They're faking so that you would use them to help with our wedding."

Akash snapped his head to Sonny. "What? Is this true?"

Sonny looked at Sangeeta, then at Akash. "It is."

"You see?" Rahul moved closer to Asha, ignoring Sangeeta's laser glare. "I would be a fool to cheat on you. They're the ones who have been taking advantage of you." He nodded at her phone. "Look at your phone."

Just then alerts and notifications went off all over the room. Sangeeta did not need to pull out her phone to see. Rahul had posted that video of her and Sonny talking about their fake relationship that night at Asha's. Her heart hammered in her chest.

After a few minutes, all eyes were on them.

It was over.

"Asha. I am sorry for all this. I assure you, I witnessed Rahul being unfaithful to you." She looked at the computer screen, willing the missing footage to magically reappear. She watched people go up and down the elevator, but no Rahul.

"We saw it last night, right?" she murmured to Sonny.

Sonny said nothing and did not make eye contact.

"You and Sonny...were faking? This whole time?" Asha looked up from her phone, even more hurt by Sangeeta, it seemed, than the potential that Rahul had cheated. She rested her watery gaze on Sangeeta. "You acted like you cared."

"I do. That's why I had to tell you about Rahul." Sangeeta stepped closer to her.

Asha stepped back, shaking her head. "You used me."

"I never meant to—" Sangeeta started, feeling the burn of tears in her own eyes. It had seemed so harmless then.

"Never meant to lie to me?" Asha's voice cracked.

"It just...happened." Sangeeta swallowed. "You saw that video of Sonny carrying me and thought we were together. I was getting maligned for being the wedding planner who ran from her own wedding. You hiring me saved my job. So, I just went with it. It was wrong. And I'm truly sorry."

Asha's eyes widened, her hurt and pain evident. "You lied to me for your *job*?"

Sangeeta had no defense. "Yes."

Asha turned her gaze to Sonny. "What about you? Why did you let her use you this way?"

"That's not exactly—"

"What did you get out of this?" Asha was softer with Sonny. "There's no way you were faking. I saw how you looked at her."

"My sister. She's trying to save the family hotel. Your wedding would have done that." He glanced at Sangeeta.

"Your sister?" Akash spoke up, barely able to make words he was so angry. "Your sister was using my sister's wedding to save her hotel? Even though she knew that Rahul was a louse?" He moved toward Sonny. Sonny did not move.

"She only found out last night," Sonny defended Reena.

"Akash. It's okay." Asha met her brother's eyes.

"No, it is not okay," he said, but he stood down.

Asha paced the room for a moment, before coming to a stop in front of Sangeeta. She hardened her gaze at Sangeeta. "I should fire you."

"Nila can take her place," Rahul said as he put his arm around Asha's waist, a victorious don't mess-with-me smirk on his face.

"That won't be necessary." Asha stiffened and stepped away from him.

"Well, someone needs to run the show, you'll be too busy."

"No. I won't. Because there will be no wedding." Asha was firm and cold.

Rahul's jaw dropped. "What?"

"You heard me. I have known for some time now, in my heart, that things were not as they seemed. But I didn't want to believe it. I wanted it to be true that you loved me—truly loved me—as I deserved. The way that Sonny so obviously loves Sangeeta. But wanting it to be true does not make it so." Asha stepped away from Rahul and stood between her siblings. "Good-bye, Rahul."

"They are lying. There's no proof!" Rahul pleaded.

"Sangeeta and Sonny came to me, knowing what

would happen to their lives if they told me this. They would not risk it for a lie." Asha straightened her shoulders and lifted her chin. "It's over, Rahul."

Rahul set his jaw and turned and left.

Silence reigned for a beat after Rahul left.

Sangeeta turned to Asha. "I'm so sorry."

Asha glared at her, her eyes narrowed. "Why? You didn't cheat on me. No wait. You just lied. As much as I want to fire you, you need to cancel everything. The wedding is off. I want my money back."

Akash exhaled deeply and wrapped his sister in huge hug. "Asha, I'm sorry."

Asha hugged her brother back. "I do hate it when you're right."

"I would give anything to be wrong right now." Akash pulled back from his sister. "I need to go." He nodded at their younger sister. "You still here?"

Nila joined them. "Of course."

Just then Reena ran in, bumping into Akash as he left. Sangeeta caught the way Akash glared at Reena. It was as if Reena had wounded him personally. Reena stepped back as if she had been struck, but quickly moved past Akash and continued toward her brother. "The wedding is off?" She looked at Sonny. "You gave her proof?"

"Of course he didn't, Reena," Sangeeta answered for him, her heart heavy with the reality. "He fixes whatever or whoever is broken. That comes first."

"Sangeeta, I did not delete—" he started.

"Why is the wedding off if there was no proof?" Reena interjected.

"Because I know everything," Asha answered. "I

know about this whole scheme with their fake relationship, trying to save her job and your family hotel. And as angry as I am about all that, I believe that Sangeeta saw what she says she saw. Rahul was unfaithful. No wedding." Asha shook her head. "I really thought we were friends. That you were helping because we would both benefit."

Sangeeta inhaled and turned to Asha. "It may take a few days, but I will close everything out for you." Without a glance at Sonny, Sangeeta started to leave, her heart heavy.

"Sangeeta," Sonny called out to her.

Before she could answer, the door jingled again. "What the hell is going on here?" Sangeeta spun around to find both of their mothers and her grandfather standing in the doorway.

"Mom!" she and Sonny and Reena all spoke in unison.

"What did I just see?" Jaya Auntie asked.

"You are faking?" Her mother pursed her lips.

"Mom, Auntie," Sangeeta started. "We can explain." She turned to Reena and Sonny.

"Yes." Sonny left Reena's side and approached the mothers.

"How could you agree to this, Sonny? What is the purpose? And why is everything online?" Jaya Auntie started. "Isn't it enough that your father may lose the hotel?"

"I was helping Reena save the hotel," Sonny insisted.

"By pretending to be in a relationship with this girl?" His mother glared at him.

"She was going to lose her job."

"That is not your problem, Sunil. You must stop fixing everybody's problems. This is how you get hurt." Jaya Auntie turned her glare in Sangeeta's direction.

"It never bothered you when it was your problems I was fixing," Sonny spoke softly, but his words hit like daggers.

Sangeeta snapped her head to him. Sonny's words were thrown at his mother, and the look of shock on Auntie's face proved that Sonny had never stood up to her before.

"Is that what you told her, Mom? That I was only interested in 'fixing' her?" Sonny said to his mother. "You can't do that."

Jaya Auntie paled, but lifted her chin defiantly. "Why not? It was the only explanation at the time."

"Sangeeta, is this true? You pretended to be in a relationship with him? Why would you do that?" her mother asked.

"She coerced Sunil so that she could save her job. Who would hire a wedding planner who ran from her own wedding?" Jaya Auntie turned to accuse at Sangeeta's mother.

"Excuse me? I believe your son did the coercing, to save your hotel. Not to mention that he benefited from an increase in business as well," Sangeeta's mother shot back. "Though it makes no difference. The faking is over. I will take my daughter back to my sister's house tonight." She set her mouth and Sangeeta could see the wheels turning in her mother's head as she made what she would call "a solid plan." "Tomorrow, I will book us tickets back to India for next week. Sangeeta will return to her job in Mumbai and this whole business will be behind us."

"No. Auntie, I'm sorry, but no one is going anywhere. We may have started out faking, but we're not faking anymore." He looked at his mother. "You can't just make decisions for everyone, Mom. I wasn't just helping her out. I'm in love with her. For real." He turned to Sangeeta. "I love you, Sangeeta. I know it in every cell in my body. I have loved you since I saw you taking ice out of your drink at the beach." He paused, gripping her in his bubble, the place where she felt most comfortable, the place where plans did not matter. "I love everything about you. I love your plans, your lists, your attention to detail. I love how you love coffee in the morning but insist on chai for work. I love how you're still making plans but are willing to go off them. I love how you keep me off-kilter, but stabilize me at the same time." He cupped her cheek with his hand. "You... You are everything I didn't know was missing from my life." He paused again, then almost whispered, "My feelings aren't fake, and they haven't ever been. I'm yours. And I want us to be together, for real."

Silence dominated the room for a moment as Sangeeta looked at him, her eyes searching his for the untruth of it all. She could not find it. All she saw was him, with his earnest brown eyes, the look on his face, naked with love for her. A small furrow formed on his forehead as he waited for her to say something.

A flurry of beeps broke the moment as Sangeeta realized her phone was blowing up. Texts from Lilliana. She glanced at them quickly. Lilliana was pissed. "I need a minute."

She ran from the crowd to Sonny's office. She'd never been so relieved to leave a room. Sonny declaring his love for her was too much. She'd rather take this call, even though she knew she was going to be fired. She listened while Lilliana went off on her before firing her. For good. Sangeeta stared at her phone, her heart heavy.

She had no job. Everyone had found out about their scheme. It had made perfect sense at the time, but now, it seemed utterly ridiculous. Her mother was back to controlling her life, taking her back to India, where she would expect Sangeeta to do exactly as she planned. There would be no wavering, no chance of the spontaneity she had come to enjoy with Sonny. Tears burned at her eyes as she considered going back to that rigid life.

More than anything, she'd be leaving Sonny behind. Her heart felt heavy just considering that possibility.

Sonny just laid out his heart to her, and she had ignored him. She had hurt Asha. Param. Her parents.

Sonny.

It was too much.

She couldn't breathe. She opened her small bag and took out the small starfish she'd held on to all this time, the mate to the one Sonny had on his desk. She placed it next to his and then quickly turned on her heel and went to the back hall. She opened the door that she had once entered.

She saw the sun and she ran.

Chapter Twenty-Eight

Sonny watched as Sangeeta grabbed her phone and headed toward his office. He knew it was her boss. She was about to get fired. He looked at his sister and found her eyes wide and panic-stricken. He hadn't seen that look on her face since she was a child, afraid of getting in trouble with their parents for something she had done. Same situation, twenty-five years later.

Everyone was talking at once. Only Asha stood off to the side, a stricken look on her face. Sonny glanced uneasily at the door Sangeeta had gone through. He started to head back to his office.

"Sonny, Sonny." Reena stopped him before he reached the hallway. "How... How did this happen?"

"Are you kidding me, Reena?" Sonny focused on his sister. "You deleted that video. You were going to let

Asha marry a cheater, just to save the hotel? Who are you?"

"*Who am I?* I am the one who has given everything she has to this hotel. Everything! Sure, you can leave when you want, just because you didn't get the position you wanted, leaving me and Papa to pick up the pieces. I was there when we had no head chef."

"Kiren was—"

"An idiot."

"An idiot our father hired. To replace me because he couldn't see—" Sonny fired up. He had done nothing but try to help. To fix things, like he always did.

"Because he wanted to stick with what he thought was working. You just wanted to come in and change things, as if you knew better. As if the time you spent in the kitchen taught you everything about a running a hotel." Reena spewed her words at him as if they'd been caged too long.

"What was I supposed to do? Stick around when Papa didn't want to do what I knew would work?" Sonny growled at his completely ungrateful sister.

"Yes." She stopped for breath. "That is exactly what you were supposed to do. You were supposed to stick around because we're family. Because you could have continued to convince Papa while Kiren was there. You could have even taught Kiren a thing or two. Because sometimes change takes time."

Sonny stared at his sister, allowing her words to really sink in. He had never considered the possibility that he could take a back seat and learn. He thought he'd already done that, washing dishes, working as a sous chef.

He had been ready—or so he had thought—to take over. To show his father what great things he could do. And when that hadn't happened, he had left. Like a toddler throwing a tantrum. His family had needed him, and he had left them as if he knew better.

"Is that why you erased the video of Rahul? To help the family? No matter the cost?"

"Damn straight. I can't be concerned with everyone's lives when I'm trying to save ours," Reena shot back.

"Yours," Sonny said softly. "You were trying to save your life. We're no different, Reena. The difference is that I now know what mistakes I made." He glanced at the back door. "Sangeeta thinks I erased it."

Reena remained stoic. If Sonny's words had made an impact, he had no idea.

"Reena!" their mother demanded. "What is going on?"

"I was trying to save Lulu's. That hotel is our life. I couldn't stand for you to sell it." Tears fell from her eyes. Sonny was torn between anger at his sister and wanting to hug away her tears. "It was my idea for Sonny and Sangeeta to fake their relationship so that Asha would hire them." Reena's eyes flicked around the room and landed on Asha. "There is video of Rahul cheating. I erased it." Reena lifted her chin to Asha. "I had to do what was best for the hotel."

Asha's eyes shone with tears. "I can't believe I thought we were friends."

Reena swallowed and pursed her lips. "I do not have friends."

Sonny looked back at the hallway leading to his office. Sangeeta had been gone a long time. Too long. His heart started racing and he turned and ran to the door, down the hallway and to his office. His heart hammered in his chest. *Please let her still be here.*

He banged open the door to his office to find it empty. He ran down the hall to the back door and opened it. The alley was empty.

His heart heavy, he returned to his office and leaned against his desk to gather himself. He glanced down as he did from time to time to look at his starfish. There was an extra starfish on his desk. She had kept it all this time.

Now, she had run.

Sonny awoke groggy from his dreams of Sangeeta and tried to focus on what he had to get done today.

He had returned to the main dining room after finding Sangeeta gone, ready to go after her, to find her. To convince her of what he already knew. That they belonged together.

"She ran again. I'm going to find her."

Reena had disappeared, but Asha had been ready to join him in his search.

"If she ran now, she will run again," his mother had said. "You give too much, beta. You always have."

Sonny had turned on his mother. "Mom. What the hell does that mean?"

"It means you have never done anything for yourself, and I know a great part of that is on me. I relied on you to help with Reena and Jai while we built Lulu's. It means that I am afraid that you feel your worth has only come from what you do for others, from what you give. And that is just not true." She looked down, and when she looked back up at him, tears swam in her eyes. "I feel responsible for you getting hurt, so I try to protect you when I can. That's why I said those things to Sangeeta. I'm sorry."

Sonny had never seen his mother apologize before. "Mom. I just need to find her."

"Leave her be." Sangeeta's grandfather had spoken. "She needs some...time." He had smiled at Sonny. "Trust me. When she is ready, she will be found. She is not ready now. Spontaneity is...new to her."

Sonny had wanted to ignore the older man. What if Sangeeta disappeared, away from him? But in the same moment he realized that if she disappeared, she disappeared. He had bared his soul to her in front of their families. She would only return on her terms.

"In the meantime, young man, you have other things to tend to," Dada had said to him before leaving. Sangeeta had always had such a soft spot for her grandfather. Sonny had seen why.

Which brought him to his chai this morning. He was going to see his father.

He dressed and was out the door quickly. Having decided to do this, he had no dread, simply the feeling that things needed to change. He had thought his father was the one to change, but maybe they both needed to.

He ran into his father leaving Lulu's just as he was entering.

"Papa."

"Sonny."

"I was just coming to see you," they spoke in unison. Then they both smiled.

Sonny spoke first. He held up a thermos. "I brought chai."

"And you are here." His father stepped aside to let him in. They walked back into the building together. Sonny followed his father and they ended up at the restaurant.

Two ceramic mugs magically appeared as they sat down, almost as if they had been conjured using a wand. Sonny poured steaming-hot chai from his thermos into both mugs.

"Papa, I—"

"Sonny, I—"

They both spoke together again.

"Me first?" Sonny asked, blowing on his chai.

His father nodded.

"I'm sorry that I left—that I let my pride get in the way of what we could have accomplished together." Sonny laid it out without preamble.

His father nodded. "You had been fixing things for this family for such a long time. It was only natural that you would want to come in and fix the hotel as well." He paused and sipped his chai. "Your mother and I came to depend on you too much. You were never really a child. That's on us."

"It was what was needed, Papa." Sonny sipped slowly. "Anyone would have done it."

His father shrugged. "But it wasn't just anyone. It was

you, our son. Your mother and I certainly could have done things differently."

"So could have I."

They sipped their chai, peace floating in the silence between them. "I wasn't brave enough to make the changes you were talking about." His father put down his mug.

Sonny stared at his father. He'd had many thoughts about his father but being "not brave" was not one of them.

"When we first started, we learned what worked and we stuck with it," his father continued. They had never talked about how Lulu's came to be. "We did not even consider that adding our background, our culture could be a benefit. We feared that it would 'other' us in a way that would not be favorable. But you and your sister seem to think that showing who we are might be positive."

"Absolutely. It's simply incorporating who we are," Sonny answered.

"It's too late, now." His father shook his head. "It's done. We owed the bank money. It was either sell or give the hotel to the bank. I have committed to the buyer as of last night. He is getting papers ready as we speak."

Sadness overcame Sonny. That hotel had been his family's life for as long as he could remember. "What will you do?"

"Your mother and I are going to take a break. Travel. We've never really been able to have a real vacation." He sounded excited at the prospect. "To be honest, selling might be a good thing for us. We've been tied to

Lulu's for so long. So has Reena. I wish she would use this sale to find her way. Her whole life is wrapped in Lulu's. It's too much."

"Reena will find her way."

"What about you?" his father asked.

"What about me?"

"Sangeeta?"

Even the name hurt him right now. He had revealed everything to her yesterday and heard nothing today. Not even a text.

"Go find her, son. Do not let her go."

"I told her everything, Papa. How I wasn't faking." He paused. "How I loved her."

"And?"

"And she left. She ran."

"Why do you think that is? Why did she run before?"

"That's just it. She ran from her wedding because a part of her knew that that wasn't the life she wanted. That she wanted something different than what she was getting herself into." Sonny felt sick to his stomach. Did that mean that she didn't want him either?

His father simply watched him.

"She was scared."

His father smiled.

"You think she's scared?"

"A lot happened. She got caught living a lie, but maybe it was more real than she had planned. And maybe that scared her, yes. She found out you loved her. She probably lost her job, too." His father drank his chai while Sonny mulled this over.

"I need to give her space." His sipped his chai, the

spices hitting just right. "Mom's right about one thing. I can't make her be with me. It has to be her choice."

His father set down his mug. "You know best." He grinned. "How about some more chai, and I'll tell you about the vacation?"

Sonny poured his father more steaming chai. "I would love that."

Chapter Twenty-Nine

When she ran, she did not go far. She mostly just walked. She just needed a few minutes to get herself together. To make herself a plan that she could live with. They would all realize she was missing but they would assume she had run again.

Her world had imploded, and instead of having an anxiety attack over it, she was going to take a minute to decide what she really wanted, before jumping into anything again.

It really wasn't a matter of time, it was simply a matter of thought. She'd had two years with Param, but still hadn't done what she wanted.

Simply because she had never asked herself.

One thing was sure.

She was ridiculously in love with Sonny Pandya.

It meant her mother had been right pairing her up

with him, but Sangeeta just did not care. That's how she knew she truly loved him. She didn't even care that her mother would be able to gloat about being right about whom she had chosen for her daughter to marry.

When he declared himself last night, she would have loved to have melted into him and forget the world. But she had been too scared to be that vulnerable again. It had hit her while she was walking that she loved him too much to risk hurting him. And she had stopped dead in her tracks.

That was bullshit.

She was simply too scared to love someone that freely. She had never allowed herself to do that before. It would have meant letting go of control.

If she had learned anything over the last month, it was that letting go of some control could be a good thing. A very good thing. Especially if that meant loving Sonny Pandya with abandon.

The first thing she did was what she should have done when she ran from Param. She put herself up in a hotel, while she started an apartment search. She loved Sonny, but she was going to need a minute. Funds were low, but she had worked on Asha's wedding, so she would be getting paid for at least part of that.

Next, she planned out a campaign for how she was going to get back into wedding planning, on her own. She'd be her own boss and build the company she'd always wanted. To that end, she texted Toral, offering her a job. Less money than with Lilliana, more responsibility, but much more autonomy.

She currently sat in front of her masi's mansion, in

an Uber. Her family was in there. She had to face them sometime.

"Thank you so much," she said to her driver, as she opened the door and faced the looming mansion as well as the thick June humidity. It was just a house.

She walked to the front door and let herself in. She arrived in the heart of the house, and for the second time in a month, everyone turned to stare at her.

"Hi."

They all spoke at one time. "Where have you been? Did you turn off your phone? I thought I was going to have to come get you again. What is going on with you?"

She took them all in. They had been worried. They had been scared. When she had turned on her phone to call the Uber, the red notification numbers had tired her out. Especially since Sonny Pandya had not contributed even one of those numbers.

She held a hand up. "I'm sorry I disappeared—again. I needed to get my head on straight—with everything that has happened."

"What you need to do is pack your bags. We have tickets to return home in two days." Her mother had been silent and had clearly been saving this for when she had Sangeeta's full attention. No matter. Sangeeta was ready for her.

"I am not going back with you, Mom." She spoke with a calm that came from finally really knowing what she wanted. "I am home."

Her mother scoffed. "That's ridiculous. You can't stay here. Where will you stay?"

"I am looking for an apartment."

"What?" Her mother's eyes bugged out.

Sangeeta never had lived on her own. She went from her father's house to the dorm at college, to living with Param. Then Sonny.

Her heart ached and lifted all at once at the thought of him—it seemed to be the glory and pain of being in love. She longed to see him, to tell him everything, but she needed to do this first. One thing at a time.

"I'm getting an apartment. In the meantime, I'll be at a hotel."

"I refuse to pay for all this." Her mother was grasping at straws.

"You're right. You're not paying for any of it." Sangeeta looked at the blank faces around her. "Asha may not be getting married, and she may be angry with me, but she is obligated to pay my fee for preparations. So, I have a little bit to keep me going while I start my own business."

"Your own business?" Her father's brow was furrowed, but the smile creeping onto his face encouraged her.

"Yes, Dad. Wedding planning. Amar and Divya are going to help me find clients. Anita is helping me with all the legal aspects, and I've signed up for a class or two to learn how to set up a business plan."

"But you ran—" her mother started.

Sangeeta waved a hand. "I did. And some people may not want my services because of that. Others either won't care, or will respect my choices. Either way, I am moving forward from that. 'Runaway bride' does not define me. Nor does 'planner.' *I* define me. I'm good at my job. Asha has agreed to vouch for me for that. It will help."

"So, you have a plan." Her mother grinned at her.

Sangeeta went to her mother. "Yes, I have a plan. But I now know that things change. Things we can't control." Like a handsome chef with the warmest brown eyes, who cooked like a god, kissed her under the stars, and wanted nothing more than to hold her tight.

Well, hopefully he still did.

"What about getting married?" her mother asked.

"I'm not ready for that right now."

Her mother's eyes widened in shock. "But then when will you have children?"

Sangeeta raised an eyebrow at her mother. Was she serious?

"You'll see. You will get sense and you'll return to us." Her mother set her mouth and nodded as if her will made it true.

It had at one time, but no more.

Sangeeta shook her head. "Mom, I have sense. My own sense." Everything she had done until this moment was to make her mother proud and happy. "I'll be living my own life now. Making my own decisions, based on what I want from life." She took her mother's hands in hers. "I love you, Mom. I just need to do things for me and not for you."

"I was only trying to guide you—"

"I know."

Sangeeta turned to the rest of her family. "Are we eating or what?"

Seema Masi and the cousins got to work getting food on the table. Sangeeta walked over to help when Dada pulled her aside.

"Beti. I am so proud of you." The gentle rumble of his voice was a balm to her soul.

Tears filled her eyes at the words. "Thank you, Dada."

He wrapped her in his comforting hug. "My daughter will come around. She just needs time."

"That's up to her. I'm done living my life for everyone else, Dada." Sangeeta smiled at him. It was freeing really. She could not remember feeling this content ever.

"What about the chef?" Dada raised an eyebrow at her.

She flushed and bit her lip.

Dada raised his hands in surrender. "Okay. You decide. You do what is best for you."

She locked her arm through his. "Come, Dada, let's eat."

Chapter Thirty

It had been three days. He hadn't heard from Sangeeta. He had no idea where she was. Tina wasn't answering his texts. He should have known better than to ask her. She was loyal to Sangeeta. He guessed she was at her masi's packing to go back to India. He packed his camping gear. He wanted to be alone. He needed to work through details of his life.

Reena had clearly gone off the deep end. The hotel was in the process of being sold to, of all people, Asha's brother, Akash Gupta. Sonny had no idea that was what Akash did, but he had seemed like a good guy.

Reena was angry. She wasn't talking to him, or anyone really, except maybe Jai. He felt for her, but this was not something he could fix. He had heard from his father that Akash had offered to keep him and Reena on as the managers, but his father was taking a well-earned break, and he'd heard that Reena was simply trying to figure out how to buy the hotel back.

He had spent more time with Jai in the past few days. The young man was a breath of fresh air. It was actually his idea that Sonny go hiking, maybe camp a night or two, before deciding what to do about Sangeeta.

Waiting her out was harder than he had thought it would be.

Sangeeta had not reached out to him. He had picked up his phone a million times to text or call her but had decided not to. She would come around if she wanted to. He wanted her to be able to determine her own rules. To be with him—or, he could hardly bear to think it— without him on her own terms.

He had already confessed his true feelings to her in front of everyone. The next step had to be hers. For her own sake.

He reached the oasis in record time and went about putting up his tents and making camp. A couple of nights here should be the distraction he needed, not to mention it might clear his head. He had closed the restaurant and given everyone time off. He needed to think about next steps. He needed to accept that he might have to find a way to get over Sangeeta.

He had just set up his telescope and settled in for the evening when he heard the noise behind him. The sun was low in the sky but had not yet set. The air was cool and devoid of the recent humidity, a rare treat in Maryland. He turned to see what was making the ruckus, half expecting an animal.

"Hey." Sangeeta popped into the clearing as if she did so every day.

"Hey." Sonny stepped back. Three days without seeing her had certainly not dimmed his memory of her, but the reality of her was breathtaking. His heart pounded in his chest as she walked into the clearing. It took all his self-control not to grab her and kiss her senseless. "I did not erase the video."

She furrowed her brow. "Of course you didn't." She pressed her lips together. "I was confused in the moment. I know you would not have done that."

"What are you doing here?" He did an internal eye roll. What kind of dork was he?

"You're here." She had removed her sunglasses in the waning sun, and looked at him from underneath her ball cap.

He said nothing.

"Meteorites tonight, right?" She nodded at the telescope.

He furrowed his brow and nodded. She was right. He could not look away from her. "I thought you were going to India."

"My mom wanted me to go to India." She looked past him. "I didn't want to go. So, I'm staying."

Something about the way she said those words was different. She was different. She was confident, stronger. In the absolute sexiest way possible. Sonny couldn't help the smile that came across his face.

"I should be on a plane right now." She half smiled, teasing him. "You didn't want to come chase me down at the airport?" She pouted at him as she removed her ball cap, freeing her hair from its ponytail.

Sonny shook his head. "I came here so I wouldn't."

She frowned as she moved closer to the camp. Closer to him.

"Did you want me to chase you down?" He felt literally frozen to his spot as she advanced on him.

"I want you to want to chase me down but not actually do it."

He sighed and shook his head at her.

She grinned at him. "So why didn't you? Chase me down."

"Because I love you."

"You *didn't* chase me down because you love me?"

"Yes. You need to decide for yourself what you want. Grand gestures are beautiful and romantic, but I wanted you to be sure what you really wanted." He needed to be sure she really wanted him.

She dropped her overstuffed backpack and came closer still. He could smell flowers and earth on her.

"I meant what I said, Sangeeta. I am in love with you. You are frustrating and stubborn and you drive me nuts sometimes. You are also one of the bravest people I know. Not to mention you are—" he waved a hand in front of her "—more beautiful, inside and out, every day. I love everything about you. I want to spend the rest of my life with you. Whether or not you want to be with me has to be your decision."

"I got an apartment."

Sonny's heart sank into his stomach.

"You came all the way up here to tell me you're moving out?" He stiffened.

"No."

"I'm asking you again. Why are you here?"

"I don't want to be without you." The words came tumbling out of her as if she had to say them fast. She inhaled and moved closer to him. Sonny was unable to move. "I've been MIA so I could get myself together, so I could breathe. I *can't* be without you. I told myself that I held back because I was afraid of hurting you. But the truth is I held back because I was afraid of needing someone like that. It scared me that I needed you like I need air to breathe. It scared me to love you with abandon. Because I do love you, Sonny Pandya. I don't know exactly when it happened, but I *know* that I love you. When you told me you weren't faking, all I wanted was to melt into your arms right then and there. You hold me tight, while letting me loose. You ground me, so I can fly. You love me for who I am, even when I'm not sure who that is sometimes."

Sonny wanted to gather her up into his arms. He held back one moment. "Why the apartment?"

"Because... I want to take my time with you. And I need to find out who I am at the same time. I want to date and go dancing and hiking and stargazing and all those things that people who are in love get to do. If we're going to do this, you need to be okay with that."

She was open, vulnerable. She had laid her heart out to him the way she never had before.

The sun was still setting, and he saw her question in the waning light. Would he take her on her terms?

He smiled at her as he leaned in to graze her lips with his. He would take her on whatever terms she set. She responded by pressing into him, a soft purr of contentment coming from her.

"I am more than okay with anything that has to do

with you, Sangeeta Parikh." He parted her lips with his mouth and kissed her properly as the light faded into darkness around them. "But I should tell you. I only have the one sleeping bag."

Epilogue

It was time. They had been together for over a year. Even though Sangeeta had her own apartment, it was barely two blocks from Sonny's and most of his things were at her place anyway.

She had relished the independence that living on her own had given her. She was confident, self-sufficient, resourceful in a way she had never been a year ago.

Sonny had patiently given her the space she needed, while still always being there for her. Her parents—even her mother—were impressed with how well her wedding planning business was going. She now had three employees, including Toral, who, it turned out, was excellent at managing the actual event and all the wild cards that showed up. Sangeeta was happy running the business and doing the beforehand work.

Sangeeta quickly cleaned and waited for Sonny to arrive. She heard his key in the lock and her stomach flipped. She went to the door and opened it.

Sangeeta had been acting strange for about a week now. Even her insistence that he come over tonight was odd. He was usually there most nights. He had started to prefer not living where he worked. The Masala Hut was doing very well, and he had been able to promote Dharm and hire another full-time sous chef, which gave Sonny a little bit of breathing room away from the kitchen.

He had no idea what was going on with her, but he suspected he was about to find out.

"Hey." He smiled at her as she opened the door as he was unlocking it.

"Hey." Her voice was too high and she was fidgety.

"Everything okay? You've been acting weird all week." Sonny walked into the apartment and kissed her.

She relaxed into their kiss and wrapped her arms around him. "I have something I wanted to ask you."

"Okay. I had something I wanted to talk to you about too," he said.

"You did?" She stepped out of his arms.

"Yes. But you go ahead." Sonny kissed her. "I'll wait."

"No." Her eyes widened. "You go first. I'll wait."

"Seriously, Sangeeta. Just say what's on your mind." What he had on his mind could wait until she had relieved herself of whatever was going on with her this week.

"I will, but let's get your thing over with," Sangeeta insisted.

"Sangeeta."

"Okay. Okay. I was just thinking." She walked away from him and paced a bit, putting her hands in her pockets, then taking them out again.

A year ago, he would have been convinced she was breaking up with him. But not now.

She inhaled and stopped to look at him. "I love you."

"You've said." He grinned at her. He would never tire of hearing it.

"I love you for who you are, and not because of all the wonderful things you do." She smiled and bit her bottom lip. "Well," she lowered her voice, and swept her gaze over him, "maybe because of some of the things you do."

"If you're going to look at me like that, you better talk fast."

She put her hands out in front of her. "Don't move. This is harder than I thought it was going to be." She mumbled. "Okay. It's just better if I show you." She turned as if to go and then turned back to him. "Just wait. Don't go anywhere."

"I'm not going anywhere," Sonny said. Life with her would never be boring.

"Okay." She turned and went to the bathroom. When she came out, she was holding a little golden retriever puppy. "This is Finn," she said, a huge grin on her face. "Finn and I were thinking that maybe you would want to give up the apartment over the restaurant and come live here, with us."

Sonny had no idea what his face showed, but his heart was thudding in his chest. He was speechless.

"Or we could find another place. And live there together. Like forever and always, I mean." Sangeeta was stumbling over her words. "Finn and I were thinking that you and I could get married."

Her eyes were huge, and it looked like she was holding her breath. "I want to spend forever in your arms, Sonny Pandya. I know it like I know the sun will rise tomorrow. There is nowhere else I'd rather be, no one else I want to share each day with. I want all your kisses to be mine. It took a minute, but I finally found my way to you, Sonny."

Sonny stood frozen to the spot and just took her in. This strong, sweet, beautiful woman whom he found his way to, who fulfilled —no exceeded—every dream he'd ever had, wanted to spend forever in his arms. Tears burned behind his eyes.

He really was a hopeless romantic.

"Sonny. Say something."

He shook his head and covered the small distance between them. He took Finn into his arms and placed a diamond ring in her hands.

He pushed up his glasses and smiled at her. He leaned in to finally touch his lips to hers. "I was thinking the same thing."

* * * * *

HARLEQUIN
PLUS

Try the best multimedia
subscription service for romance
readers like you!

Read, Watch and Play.

Experience the easiest way to get
the romance content you crave.

Start your **FREE TRIAL** at
<u>www.harlequinplus.com/freetrial</u>.